THE SEA KING'S LADY

SEVEN KINGDOMS TALE 2

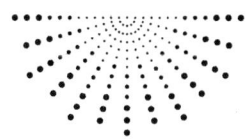

S.E. SMITH

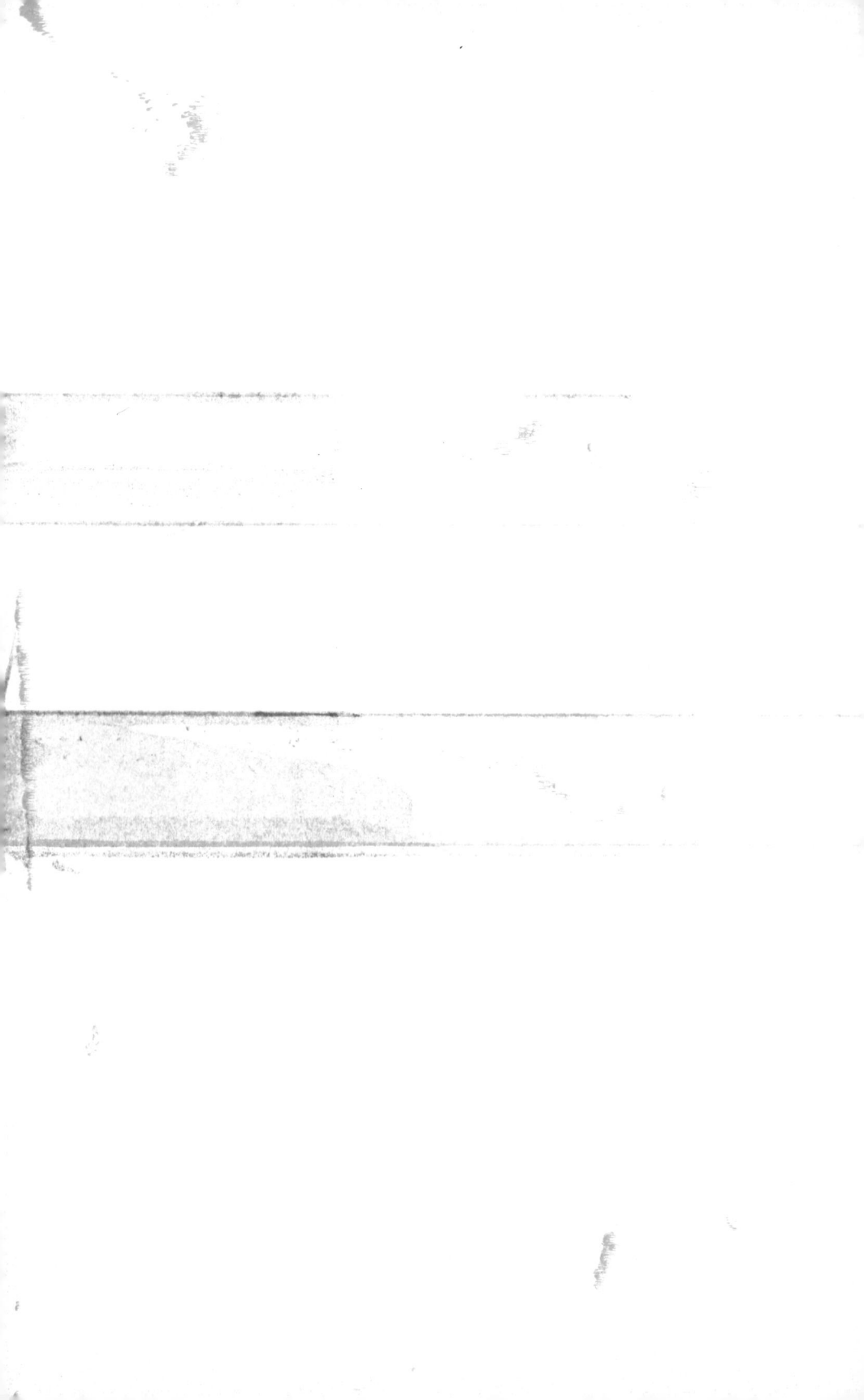

ACKNOWLEDGMENTS

I would like to thank my husband Steve for believing in me and being proud enough of me to give me the courage to follow my dream. I would also like to give a special thank you to my sister and best friend, Linda, who not only encouraged me to write, but who also read the manuscript. Also to my other friends who believe in me: Julie, Debbie, Christel, Sally, Jolanda, Lisa, Laurelle, and Narelle. The girls that keep me going!

And a special thanks to Paul Heitsch, David Brenin, Samantha Cook, Suzanne Elise Freeman, and PJ Ochlan—the awesome voices behind my audiobooks!

—S.E. Smith

The Sea King's Lady: A Seven Kingdoms Tale 2
Copyright © 2017 by S. E. Smith
First E-Book Published December 2017
Cover Design by Melody Simmons

ALL RIGHTS RESERVED: This literary work may not be reproduced or transmitted in any form or by any means, including electronic or photographic reproduction, in whole or in part, without express written permission from the author.

All characters and events in this book are fictitious or have been used fictitiously, and are not to be construed as real. Any resemblance to actual persons living or dead, actual events, or organizations are strictly coincidental and not intended by the author.

Summary: A young woman searching for her missing friend tries to save the life of a young boy only to find herself in a magical underwater kingdom in a far off world.

ISBN (kdp paperback) 978-1985581203
ISBN (BN paperback) 9781078746892
ISBN (eBook) 978-1-944125-19-6

Romance (love, explicit sexual content) | Action/Adventure | Fantasy (Urban) | Fantasy Dragons & Mythical Creatures | Contemporary | Paranormal

Published by Montana Publishing, LLC
& SE Smith of Florida Inc. www.sesmithfl.com

CONTENTS

Prologue	1
Chapter 1	9
Chapter 2	18
Chapter 3	24
Chapter 4	30
Chapter 5	39
Chapter 6	50
Chapter 7	60
Chapter 8	73
Chapter 9	83
Chapter 10	94
Chapter 11	101
Chapter 12	109
Chapter 13	121
Chapter 14	130
Chapter 15	141
Chapter 16	148
Chapter 17	156
Chapter 18	166
Chapter 19	172
Chapter 20	183
Chapter 21	190
Epilogue	200
Additional Books	210
About the Author	213

THE SEVEN KINGDOMS REFERENCE

Isle of the Elementals – created first
King Ruger and Queen Adrina
- Can control earth, wind, fire, water, and sky. Their power diminishes slightly when they are off their isle.
- Goddess' Gift: The Gem of Power.

Isle of the Dragons – created second
King Drago
- Controls the dragons.
- Goddess' Gift: Dragon's Heart.

Isle of the Sea Serpent – created third
King Orion
- Can control the Oceans and Sea Creatures.
- Goddess' Gift: Eyes of the Sea Serpent.

Isle of Magic – created fourth
King Oray and Queen Magika
- Their magic is extremely powerful but diminishes slightly when they are off their island.
- Goddess' Gift: The Orb of Eternal Light.

Isle of the Monsters – created fifth for those too dangerous or rare to stay on the other Isles
Empress Nali can see the future.
- Goddess' Gift: The Goddess' Mirror.

Isle of the Giants – created sixth
King Koorgan
- Giants can grow to massive sizes when threatened – but only if they are off their isle.

- Goddess' Gift: The Tree of Life.

Isle of the Pirates – created last for outcasts from the other Isles
The Pirate King Ashure Waves, Keeper of Lost Souls
- Collectors of all things fine. Fierce and smart, pirates roam the Isles trading, bargaining, and occasionally helping themselves to items of interest.
- Goddess' Gift: The Cauldron of Spirits.

Characters:
Magna: half witch/half sea people she is Orion's distant cousin on his father's side
Drago: King of the Dragons.
Carly Tate: Banking Associate from Yachats, Oregon
Orion: King of the Sea People
Jenny Ackerly: School Teacher and Carly's best friend
Dolph: Orion's 8 year old son from his first marriage
Juno: Orion's 5 year old son from his first marriage
Shamill: Orion's first wife – deceased.
Kapian: Orion's Captain of the Guard and best friend
Kelia: Orion's elderly nursemaid
Coralus: Kelia's husband, a royal guard & mentor to Orion and Kapian
Kell: Magna's father
Seline: Magna's mother
Ashure Waves: King of the Pirates
Bleu LaBluff: Ashure's Second-in-Command
Nali: Empress of the Monsters
Ross Galloway: Fisherman from Yachats, Oregon
Mike Hallbrook: Detective for Yachats, Oregon Police Department
Koorgan: King of the Giants
Isha: Captain of the Guard for the King and Queen of the Isle of Magic
Magika: Queen of the Isle of Magic
Cyan: Female Cyclops: Boost's mate
Boost: Male Cyclops: Cyan's mate
Meir: Minotaur

SYNOPSIS

Clutching the material of the gown in her hands, she lifted it just far enough to make sure she didn't step on it before raising her chin and straightening her shoulders. She was going to do this.

"I've totally lost my mind," she said, staring at the door and willing her legs to work.

"Completely, so you have nothing to worry about," Kelia informed her.

Jenny can't bring herself to give up the search for Carly, even after all this time. Orion can't stop the Sea Witch from using his child to seal the fate of the merpeople. An unlikely alliance between Jenny and Orion could change everything, but what will it take survive the evil lurking in the depths of the ocean?

Jenny Ackerly is devastated when her best friend disappears without a trace. During her latest search for Carly, her determination turns to horror when she sees a young boy running from an empty beach into the freezing sea. When the boy doesn't resurface, Jenny's protective instincts ignite and she rushes to save the child from certain death, swimming farther and deeper than she ever would have on her own, until she is caught in a powerful undertow. When Jenny resurfaces, she is in a magical, underwater world.

Orion is the powerful ruler of the Isle of the Sea Serpent and protector of the oceans, but time is running out for him. For hundreds of years, the Eyes of the Sea Serpent have been in his family's possession, giving them power over the oceans, and now they have been stolen! Meanwhile, his oldest son's bargain with the Sea Witch threatens to seal the fate of the merpeople—and possibly that of the Seven Kingdoms. The situation seems hopeless—until a fiery female from another world appears....

PROLOGUE

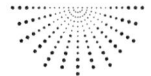

 ive years earlier:

"Your Majesty," one of the guards urgently called to Orion.

Orion turned with a frown. He nodded at Kapian, his Captain of the Guard, to wait for him. They needed to review the damage caused by a minor earthquake that had struck three hours earlier, develop a plan of action to help those affected, and send support crews to begin repairs.

He and Kapian had just returned from a scouting mission offshore. The quake had rippled along the rocky floor of the ocean, opening a crevice that almost sucked them into it. They had hastily returned to the Isle of the Sea Serpent after they realized that the quake would probably impact the island as well.

There was no damage to the underwater city when they returned there, but he had received reports of some damage to the city above. Though the intensity of the earthquake had been relatively minor, he was concerned about the possibility of a Tsunami causing further damage to the upper kingdom. The new buildings were designed to withstand much stronger quakes, but there were also many older structures that would be vulnerable. His frown deepened when he realized who had called out to him. York was his wife's personal guard and was normally never far from her side.

"Is there a problem?" he demanded, noting the worried expression in York's eyes.

"It is the Queen, Your Majesty. She was hurt in the earthquake," York stated.

"Orion, do you want me to…," Kapian said, turning to gaze at Orion.

Orion shook his head at Kapian's sympathetic tone. "Find out if anyone else has been injured for me, Kapian, while I see to Shamill," Orion ordered before he turned to face York again. "Where is she?"

"In her chambers, Your Majesty," York replied.

Orion brushed past the guard and strode toward his wife's chambers. Palace guards straightened to attention as he passed, but he ignored them. His thoughts were on Shamill.

"Your Majesty," York called from behind him.

Orion impatiently turned to the guard, his hand on the door handle to Shamill's living quarters. He waited for York to catch up. His lips tightened when he saw an expression of grief in the man's eyes.

"What is it?" he demanded.

"I should warn you…," York said before his voice faded and he glanced at the door. "The Queen's injuries were most grievous. I should have protected her better. Please accept my deepest regrets, Your Majesty."

Orion didn't wait to hear York's next words. He didn't need to—the man's expression told him that Shamill's injuries must have been worse than he had first thought. Turning around, he pushed open the door. Three healers turned toward him when he entered the room and bowed in respect. They did not speak as he continued through the sitting room to Shamill's bedroom.

He paused for a brief second in the doorway. In addition to the healers conversing in the sitting room, there were three women in the room with his wife. The first was one of Shamill's Ladies-in-Waiting who was brushing a damp cloth across Shamill's pale forehead. Shamill lay against the pristine white sheets, her skin almost the same color. He moved his gaze to the second woman who stood near the window. This woman held a small bundle in her arms and was swaying back and forth.

"Your Majesty," the third woman, Kelia, murmured with a respectful bow of her head.

Kelia had been his nursemaid when he was young and had been attending to Shamill during the later months of her pregnancy. His gaze moved over Kelia's lined face before shifting to Shamill's peaceful one. He hadn't missed the sorrow in the older woman's eyes.

"How is she?" he asked in a low voice.

"Not good, Your Majesty. Her highness was walking along the upper cliffs when the earthquake occurred. A portion of the retaining wall along one of the walking paths collapsed on top of her, trapping her," Kelia explained in a trembling voice. "Her guard found her and called for assistance."

"The babe…," Orion hesitantly asked.

"Your son survived, but keeping him alive until he could be born has cost the Queen her life," Kelia replied.

Orion walked over to the edge of the bed. Shamill's Lady-in-Waiting rose and silently walked over to the window. Orion sank down onto the bed next to his wife.

In the background, he heard Kelia murmur quietly to the young woman standing next to the window. The young woman holding his son handed the infant to Kelia before she and Shamill's Lady-in-

Waiting quietly exited the room. Kelia walked over and held out the infant to him. Orion tenderly scooped the baby into his arms.

"I will be outside the door if you need my assistance," Kelia murmured.

Orion nodded and gazed down at the round, rosy cheeks of the sleeping infant. He lifted a finger and gently ran it down the baby's cheek. Almost immediately, the baby turned his head and opened his mouth.

"He… is… well?" Shamill asked in a voice that was barely audible.

Orion moved his gaze to Shamill. Her eyes were open, but he could see the shadows of death in them. Her gaze was no longer sharp and clear. The light that usually glimmered in her eyes was now barely visible.

"Yes, he is," Orion said, adjusting the baby in his arms so Shamill could see him.

A hint of a smile curved her lips before it faded. She winced and drew in a shaky breath. Her eyelids fluttered and closed for a moment before she forced them open again. Their gazes locked, and a sense of sorrow filled him. While he and Shamill had never been in love with each other, they were good friends. He respected her quiet grace and gentle soul.

"Dolph…," Shamill whispered.

"He is safe," Orion reassured her.

"Let me… just one… time… before…."

Orion gently laid the baby on Shamill's chest. He instinctively reached out to catch the tear that escaped from the corner of her eye. She moved her left hand, but she was too weak to lift it. Reaching down, he cupped it and placed her cold fingers against their son's warm cheek.

"What… name…?" she asked in a threadbare voice.

"Juno. His name is Juno, just like you insisted," Orion said with a small, sad smile.

"Juno...," Shamill whispered.

Orion grasped her hand when it started to slide. Drawing her cold fingers to his lips, he pressed a kiss to the tips. His gaze remained fixed on her face as the last of the light swirled and faded in her eyes. Juno's faint cry pierced him, it was as if the child could feel that his mother was gone.

"May your journey bring you happiness, Shamill. I will protect both of our sons and the kingdom," Orion said in a quiet voice.

He bent forward and pressed a kiss to her forehead before he gently scooped the fretting baby into his arms. Grief swept through him as he rose from the bed. Turning, he saw Kelia standing just outside the open doorway. She started forward with her arms out, but he shook his head.

"Where is Dolph?" he asked.

"The young lord is in the garden with his nursemaid," Kelia replied.

"I want you to find a nursemaid for Juno. Tell her to meet me in the garden in ten minutes," Orion ordered.

"Yes, Your Majesty," Kelia said with a bow of her head.

Orion walked through the sitting room and out through the balcony doors. Shamill had insisted on a first-floor apartment when they married as she feared heights and enjoyed being near the gardens. His own apartments were located in the West tower. He preferred to be able to look out over the ocean when he was on the isle.

Walking across the wide, covered balcony, Orion descended the steps and continued along the stone path. He instinctively shielded the baby in his arms as he walked through the garden. Even though the sun was low on the horizon, he knew the babe would be sensitive to light. He paused under a nearby tree and listened. He smiled when he heard the squeal of his eldest son's voice, followed by a splash.

"Master Dolph, you are not to get wet! Dinner will be soon," the nursemaid sharply scolded.

Orion walked down the path to a small stream that ran through the garden. Dolph sat in the middle of it, laughing and splashing. His eldest son was already a handful and, if the frustrated expression on the woman's face was anything to go by, it appeared he would be assigning a new nursemaid before long.

"I will see to him," Orion said in a dismissive tone.

The woman turned in surprise. Orion saw her gaze move to the baby in his arms before returning to his face. She looked shaken.

"Yes, Your Majesty. I… My heart goes with the Queen," she said, lightly touching her fingers to her chest near her heart.

"My gratitude for your sympathy," Orion replied before he focused his attention on his oldest son. "Dolph, come here."

"Father, I can make the water dance!" Dolph giggled, wiggling his fingers.

Orion watched as the water rose and swirled at his son's command. There was no denying that Dolph would be a very powerful ruler one day. He smiled at his eldest son's delight. Life continued.

"Very good, son. Come, meet your new brother," Orion said as he walked over to a stone bench under a tree and sat down.

"Can I teach him to make the water dance?" Dolph asked, climbing up the bank.

Orion chuckled. "When he is older," he promised.

Dolph hurried over to his father. He paused and gazed down at the small bundle in Orion's arms before looking up at his father with a frown. Another smile tugged at the corner of Orion's mouth at the perplexed expression on his son's face.

"He is small," Dolph said, gazing down at his brother again.

"So were you when you were his age," Orion gently explained.

"Can I touch him?" Dolph asked, looking up at his father.

"Yes, but be gentle," Orion replied, readjusting Juno so his elder brother could see him better.

"Mother went away. Didn't she want to be with us anymore?" Dolph asked, sliding his finger along Juno's cheek.

"Who told you about your mother?" Orion demanded, looking intently at his son.

Dolph giggled when Juno opened his mouth and tried to suck on his finger. Orion's mouth tightened in annoyance. It was his place to explain what had happened to Shamill. If the nursemaid had said anything....

"The water," Dolph replied. "Will he get teeth?"

"The water...?" Orion asked with a frown.

Dolph nodded and looked up at his father. "The water told me that Mother had returned to her. She said not to be sad because we would have a new mother one day who would love us just as much," he replied. "Can I go play in the water again?"

Orion nodded, stunned by his son's statement. The sound of approaching footsteps drew his attention. Kapian, Kelia, and a young girl paused briefly near the path leading to the stone bench where he sat.

Orion rose to his feet as they approached. Kelia reached out for Juno, who was beginning to fuss again. He handed the newborn to her.

"We will see to his care, Your Majesty," Kelia said. "This is my granddaughter, Karin."

"Thank you, Kelia," Orion absently replied.

The realization of what had happened began to sink in as he watched Karin cradle Juno in her arms before she and Kelia turned and walked away. Orion turned to watch Dolph play in the water. Even at the tender age of two and a half, his eldest was showing the power of his birthright as Prince of the Sea People. Dolph would need a firm hand to guide him.

Orion glanced at his friend, Kapian. "I want to know exactly what happened. Shamill was terrified of heights. She would never have traveled along the cliff path," he stated in a grim voice.

"I will have a full report for you as soon as possible. I've also ordered construction of temporary safety railings along the cliffs. It will take time to repair all of the damage, but we will do everything we can to ensure such a tragedy does not occur again," Kapian promised.

Orion nodded, lost in thought. There was too much to do at the moment to give in to the grief pressing on him. Shamill's death would not only leave a void in his life, but also in the kingdom.

CHAPTER ONE

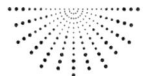

*P*resent day—Yachats, Oregon:

Jenny Ackerly's heart was telling her that her best friend was not dead—even as her head argued the opposite. The long, winding road through the redwoods along the Oregon coast felt a lot like her life over the last two years since Carly's disappearance—a never-ending journey of twists and turns. She was ready for the road of life to straighten out a little so she could see where in the hell it was taking her.

"She isn't dead. I would know, damn it!" she cursed under her breath.

The burning in her eyes and the sudden need to sneeze warned Jenny that she was about to start crying. She always did when she got within five miles of Yachats State Park.

She kept her eyes on the road as she leaned over the passenger's seat, opened the glove box of her Subaru Outback, and pulled out a handful of napkins she had collected from various restaurants. She had already used up the last few tissues she had left from her trip here three months ago.

She wiped the escaping tears from her cheeks before loudly blowing her nose into the damp napkin. Reaching over, she stuffed the used napkin in the empty tissue box. Next, she twisted the knob on the radio and cranked up the volume. Another loud, shuddering curse escaped her when a new song started, and she recognized it as one of Carly's favorites. Of course, that really turned on the waterworks. Pressing the button, she turned off the radio.

Grabbing another napkin, she dabbed at the tears threatening to blind her. If she started crying too hard, she would have to pull over onto the shoulder of the road. It wouldn't be the first time she had been forced to park until she could compose herself. Unfortunately, the only thing crying did was make her face red and eat up precious time she could be using to find out what had happened to Carly. Blowing her nose once more, she angrily stuffed the used tissue into the rapidly filling box.

"I swear, when I find out who did this to you, Carly, I'm going to toast their ass. I'll rip them apart, put them back together, ask them how it feels, and do it all over again," Jenny vowed, gripping the steering wheel so tightly her knuckles were white. "If they made you su… suff… suffer at all, I'll bury them in a fire ant bed in the middle of the desert and watch the ants devour them while sipping on an icy lemonade."

Okay, she wouldn't really, but she could imagine it. Yes, she could be a bit bloodthirsty when it came to anyone who hurt her friends. Jenny decided it was just part of having red hair. She was known to have a nice, even temperament—until someone did something to piss her off. Then, the temper she inherited from her dad came through in all its blazing glory.

Jenny slowed and turned on her blinker when she saw the exit up ahead. She turned left into the entrance to Yachats State Park, and followed the road to the ranger's booth. A light drizzle had begun, but that wouldn't stop her from her mission. Rain or shine, cold or fog, she would follow the last trail that Carly took. She would search every tiny inch of it in the hopes that maybe the weather and time had exposed some clue that all the police and volunteers might have overlooked two years ago after she reported her friend missing.

"How many?" the ranger asked when she pulled up to the window.

"Just one," Jenny replied, handing him her annual pass.

The ranger studied it for a moment before looking at her. Jenny could feel his gaze move over her face. It didn't take long for recognition to hit.

"You're the girl who keeps searching for the one that went missing, aren't you?" the ranger asked, leaning on the window sill.

Jenny grimaced and nodded. "Her name is Carly Tate. Has anyone found anything?" she asked, holding her hand out for the pass.

"Nothing. There have been a few people who still come out on occasion to look, but it's been a while," the ranger replied with an inviting smile. "I'll be off at three if you'd like me to go with you."

Jenny pursed her lips together and shook her head. "That's okay. I don't have much time today," she lied.

The ranger's expression drooped and he shrugged. "Be careful. There has been some erosion along the trail leading down to the cove," he said, handing her the pass and a parking permit. "Keep an eye out for sudden weather changes. Fog and rain can move in quickly at this time of year, making visibility difficult."

"I will, thank you."

Jenny didn't wait for the rest of his memorized spiel. Having grown up in this area, she was aware of the sudden changes in weather and how to deal with them. Pulling up on the power button to close the window, she gave the car a little more gas than she meant to and felt the jar of the speed bump. With a grimace, she eased up on the pedal and slowly pulled away.

Once she was out of sight of the ranger station, she accelerated again. She followed the long, winding road and turned at the appropriate signs without having to read them. She knew where she was going. Pulling into the parking space, she noticed with satisfaction that there was only one other car in the parking lot, and it looked like the owners of it were leaving.

Jenny sat in her car and waited as the man and the woman argued over the map they were looking at. Tapping her fingers on the steering wheel, she impatiently resisted the urge to get out and ask the couple if they needed some help. Turning the engine off, she undid her seatbelt and turned to reach into the back seat for her jacket.

Straightening in her seat, she blinked back the tears that threatened again and released a deep, shuddering breath when the car next to her finally pulled away. Opening the door, she slid out, pulled on her jacket, and zipped it up before she closed the door. Out of habit, she gazed around her for a moment before she locked the door and pocketed her car keys.

Ever since Carly disappeared two years ago, Jenny hadn't felt safe. She had moved away from the small coastal community of Yachats, Oregon, over a year ago in an effort to get on with her life. So far, she had to admit she wasn't doing a very good job of it.

Jenny slowly walked up the trail and paused at a fork. The path ahead of her did a loop through the forest and along the mountain. The one to the right lead down to the cove and beach area.

She quickly dismissed that area. Carly had left a map of the park in her car with the longest path highlighted in green and the words 'I can do this' written next to it. Jenny smiled when she remembered the added note 'ice cream' written and circled in black at the end of the trail.

Shoving her hands in her pockets, she continued past the sign pointing to the beach. She breathed in the rich smells of evergreens, moist soil, and frigid sea air as she walked. She scanned the path as her mind focused on what it would have been like for Carly.

"She would have been grumbling a lot," Jenny reflected out loud after a mile along the trail.

Pausing to look around, she sighed. Tall trees, thick ferns, and sloping ravines greeted her intense gaze. It was possible that Carly had stumbled, rolled down the side into the ferns, hit her head on a rock, and then was swallowed by the thick vegetation. *Carly was known for her clumsiness. It's possible that there was no foul play beyond bad luck*, Jenny silently admitted to herself.

"Surely someone would have found her if that had happened," Jenny murmured before continuing up the narrow track.

Twilight was beginning to settle by the time Jenny drove back into town. It turned out to be another fruitless one with no new leads. She had one more stop before she'd call it a day.

Slowing down as she entered town, she glanced around for a parking space. Now that summer was starting and people were taking off for their vacation, there were quite a few tourists in town. She breathed a sigh of relief when she saw two open parking spots in front of the local police station.

Turning on her blinker, she waited for several cars to pass before pulling into one of the empty spots. A quick glance at the clock told her it was later than she'd thought. She shifted the gearshift to park and turned off the engine. Staring straight ahead, she could see a woman behind the desk. It looked like she was getting ready to leave.

Jenny didn't waste any time undoing her seatbelt and pushing open the car door. She hoped that the new detective she had been talking to for the past couple of months was on duty. She didn't see him through the window, but there was a light shining from an office down the hall. Slamming the car door, she locked it, and strode across the sidewalk.

She pushed open the door just as the woman behind the desk slid the strap of her purse onto her shoulder.

"Can I help you?" the woman asked, looking up at Jenny as she entered.

Jenny smiled, remembering the woman from the last time she was here. She hoped Patty would remember her as well. It took a moment before recognition hit. Patty threw a quick glance over her shoulder.

"Mike, the lady about the missing person is back," Patty called out, walking around the desk. "He'll be with you in a moment. He is on the phone."

"Thank you," Jenny said with an appreciative smile before she stepped to the side.

"No problem. I have to pick up my son. Have a good night," Patty said with an easy smile before pulling open the door and stepping outside.

Jenny could hear the sound of a man's voice speaking quietly in the background. She turned and walked over to stand near the front window and stare blindly out at the street. She didn't want to give the impression she was eavesdropping on his conversation. Lost in thought, she didn't realize he was finished until he spoke behind her.

"Good afternoon, Miss Ackerly," Mike Hallbrook's rich, smooth voice greeted.

Jenny turned to face the tall, handsome man who looked to be in his early thirties. Mike Hallbrook had one of those quiet, calm demeanors that drew you in and gave you a sense of security. The undeniable authority in his posture told her that while he may appear relaxed, he was always on alert.

She reached up to tuck a stray hair behind her ear and nibbled her lip in indecision. She felt slightly guilty for stopping by when it was so late. In a small town like Yachats, there wasn't a huge need to have someone with Mike's expertise on duty after hours unless there was a major crime. Still, she had to ask.

Jenny gave Mike a tired, apologetic smile. After ten hours of hiking and searching every nook and cranny along the trail, she was exhausted and disheveled. She was just thankful he didn't appear to care that she was here so late.

"Hello, Detective Hallbrook. Thank you for seeing me," she responded.

Mike Hallbrook nodded his head. "Anytime. What can I do for you?" he asked.

Jenny could feel his scrutiny. She could just imagine what he was seeing—damp and wrinkled clothing, dark circles under her eyes, windswept hair, and red cheeks. She looked like something that had washed up on the shore. With a weary smile, she drew in a tired breath before she released it.

"I was checking to see if there were any updates on Carly Tate's missing person's case," she said.

"Nothing since the last time you came in three months ago," Mike responded in a compassionate tone.

"Oh... The... The case hasn't been closed, has it?" she asked.

Mike Hallbrook took in the tired, disheveled appearance of the woman standing across from him. A moment of regret flashed through him that he couldn't give her the answer to the question she had been asking for two years—what happened to her friend. The fate of Carly Tate was still unknown—a cold case for their small town.

When the Yachats Police Department receptionist, Patty, had called out, as she left for the night, that the girl who was looking for the missing woman was back, Mike didn't need the case number to know who Patty was talking about. There were not a lot of unsolved crimes in the area.

"No, the case won't be closed until we know what happened to your friend. Unfortunately, there isn't a lot to go on. I'm continuing to investigate leads. Do you have any new information?" he asked.

Jenny shook her head and wrapped her arms around her waist. "No. Did you ever get a chance to talk to Ross Galloway again? He was the last guy Carly dated. I've been meaning to ask but kept forgetting," she asked.

Mike nodded. "Yes. He has a solid alibi for the day Carly disappeared," he replied.

Mike took a step closer when tears welled up in Jenny's eyes. It was times like this that he hated being a cop. He watched as she bowed her head and pulled a tissue from her pocket. He heard her draw in a shuddering breath before she looked up at him. A faint smile curved his lips when he saw the determination in her expression.

"I left my phone number with your receptionist the last time I was here. Can you please call me if you find out anything?" she asked.

"I'll make sure it's the same number I have marked in the file. If we find anything, I'll be sure to contact you," he promised.

"Thank you," she said, turning toward the door.

"Any time. If you think of anything that might help locate your friend, please don't hesitate to call," Mike added.

"I won't. I plan to be here for the rest of the week. Thank you again for not giving up on Carly," Jenny said, glancing up at him when he reached around her to open the door.

"We'll bring her home," he responded in a quiet tone.

Jenny's eyes glistened with unshed tears. She nodded and stepped through the opened door. Mike watched her hurry across the sidewalk to a dark red Subaru parked out front. He stood in the doorway, lost in thought.

The case puzzled him. From the few conversations he'd had with Carly's parents, he'd gathered that they had already accepted that their daughter was dead and would probably never be found. The cold, disconnected resignation in their voices was completely opposite to Jenny Ackerly's grief. During his investigation he had learned that Carly had been a warm, cheerful young woman who got along with everyone. Hell, even Ross Galloway shook his head and said he couldn't see anyone harming Carly.

"She is dangerous enough to herself," Ross had said in exasperation.

When Mike had pressed Ross about what he meant, he discovered Carly was known as a lovable, but klutzy woman. Ross' description of her setting his boat on fire—a very minor fire, Ross had hastily clarified —helped Mike understand some of the other references made about Carly by other people.

"Knowing Carly, she probably got lost in the woods or fell off a cliff," Ross had said with a shrug. "It wouldn't be the first time."

It was a possibility, but something told Mike it was more than a simple act of getting lost. The numerous search teams would have found something. If Carly had fallen from the cliff, the tides would have washed her up on the shore because of the way the cove was shaped. He had already checked the area.

Mike blinked when a resident drove by and honked the horn in greeting. He automatically lifted his hand to wave and realized he was still standing in the open doorway of the small police station. Shaking his head in resignation, he stepped back, closed the door, and locked it.

He was supposed to be off now. Instead, he turned back toward his office. Maybe he'd take another look at the file and see if there was something he'd missed. After all, it wasn't like people just vanished off the face of the earth! There had to be a clue somewhere that would point him in the right direction of what had happened to Carly Tate.

CHAPTER TWO

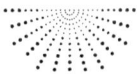

*J*enny backed out of the parking space and turned south. She had only gone a block when her stomach rumbled. Grimacing at the reminder that she hadn't eaten all day, she considered her options: stop at the grocery store or stop at one of the restaurants.

She quickly decided that fighting the crowds at the grocery store and then having to prepare something to eat was more than she could handle at the moment. That decision made, she focused on where to stop. She really didn't feel like going alone to one of the nicer waterfront restaurants. What she really wanted was a nice cold beer and a platter of fish and chips.

Turning right at the stoplight, she headed for one of the pubs that was popular with the locals. Five minutes later, she was pulling into the parking lot of the Underground Pub. It didn't look like much on the outside, but it had great food, cold beer, live music, and a nice ambiance.

Grabbing her purse and jacket from the passenger seat, she opened the door and slid out. The smell of the ocean mixed with the fragrant aroma of food made her stomach growl again in anticipation.

Jenny shut and locked the car door. Seagulls squawked as they landed on the docks in the hope of finding a meal from the fishermen cleaning their daily catch or from a generous patron willing to share a leftover French fry or two. A brisk breeze swirled around her, and she quickly pulled her jacket on when it sent a chill through her. Shouldering her handbag, she crossed the uneven gravel of the parking lot to the entrance of the pub.

Jenny pulled the door open and stepped into the dim interior. She paused as her eyes adjusted. Glancing around, she saw the band equipment set up along one wall. Wooden tables laden with condiments and scarred but sturdy chairs filled the interior to the point that Jenny was amazed the waitress could squeeze between them.

It was still early in the evening, and close to half of the tables were already filled with patrons. Jenny nodded to the waitress when she called out for her to sit wherever she wanted. Squeezing between two tables, Jenny made her way toward one in the back near the large set of double doors leading outside to the patio seating.

She slid into an empty seat with her back to the dark hallway leading to the bathrooms. From this vantage point, she could see the docks outside but was still far enough away from the band to keep from going deaf when they started playing. She glanced at her phone—almost eight o'clock. The band started at nine. If she were lucky, she would be out of here before then. Otherwise, her head would be hurting a lot more than it was at the moment.

"My name's Dorothy. What can I get you to drink, darling?" Dorothy asked with a friendly smile.

"Beer, whatever local beer you have on tap is fine. I don't need a menu. I'll take the fish basket with fries and coleslaw," Jenny said.

Dorothy tucked the menu she was about to hold out back under her arm and grinned. "The two piece or three piece, sugar?" Dorothy asked.

"Two is fine," Jenny replied.

"I'll bring you some chips and salsa," Dorothy replied with another smile.

"Thank you," Jenny responded.

She watched Dorothy take another drink order on her way back to the kitchen. Turning her head, Jenny stared out of the glass doors, lost in thought. She absently watched three older men as they stood around chatting. She smiled when she saw several pelicans and seagulls vying for a spot near the cleaning table.

"Here you go, sweetie," Dorothy said, placing the frosted glass of beer and the plate with the salsa and chips down in front of her.

"Thank you," Jenny replied with a grateful smile.

Dorothy stood and placed her hands on her hips. "Haven't I seen you here before?" she asked with a frown.

Jenny paused as she reached for the glass of beer. "Yes," she replied, not really wanting to talk.

Dorothy nodded and smiled. "I thought so. Your food will be right out. We have a great band tonight, so be sure to stick around," she said before moving to a new group of people who came in.

Sure enough, Dorothy stopped by a few minutes later with her fish platter. Jenny picked at the food, eating more because she knew she needed to than because she was hungry. After the first few bites, her stomach stopped rumbling, and she lost interest in the delicious meal.

A wave of weariness suddenly washed through her and she decided she'd done enough damage to the food in front of her. She was wiping her hands clean with a paper towel when the chair across the table from her was pulled out and a man wearing a dark brown leather jacket, white T-shirt, and faded jeans sat down. Jenny glanced up, the sharp retort on her lips faded when she recognized the grim-faced man. Straightening, she placed the paper towel down next to her plate and scowled at him.

"I didn't invite you to sit at my table," she said in a sharp tone.

Ross Galloway lifted the bottle of beer in his hand and took a long swig, not responding to her blunt statement. Jenny could feel her temper starting to rise. If Ross wasn't careful, he'd be wearing that bottle upside his head. Her eyes narrowed when he lowered his hand and put the bottle back on the table.

"I didn't have anything to do with Carly's disappearance," he said.

Jenny shrugged and sat back in her chair. "I heard you had an alibi," she replied.

"I liked her. She was a bit too dangerous to be around, but I liked her," Ross said, leaning forward and resting his arms on the table.

Jenny returned his steady gaze with one of her own. He didn't glance away, his expression compassionate and intense. Ross might be a jerk, but he'd never struck her as being dangerous.

"She could be hazardous at times," Jenny reluctantly agreed.

Ross nodded and relaxed, leaning back in his chair. "Have you heard if the authorities have found anything more?" he asked.

"No, they haven't," Jenny replied.

They both sat in silence for several minutes, each lost in their own thoughts. Jenny watched Ross. He absently played with his bottle of beer. A slight frown creased his brow, and he looked like he was trying to decide if he should say something else.

"Do you…."

"I guess…."

They both spoke at the same time. Ross released a long sigh and motioned for her to continue. Jenny twisted her lip in sardonic amusement.

"I was going to say, I guess I should be going. It's been a long day, and I'd like to do another search tomorrow," Jenny said.

"Yeah, well, I was going to ask if you wanted any help. I know that the cops have searched. It's been so long now, I doubt there is anything left out there. Carly's bones would either be scattered to hell and back or gone if she fell into the sea," Ross muttered.

"She's not dead," Jenny retorted as a flash of anger and grief rose inside her.

Pushing her chair back, she stood up. She pulled some money from her pocket and counted out enough for her bill. She placed it on the rectangular plastic tray that Dorothy left with her meal.

"Aw hell, Jenny. I didn't mean to upset you," Ross said, standing up.

"She's not dead. I would know," Jenny stubbornly insisted, lifting a hand to brush her hair back from her face.

"It's been a long time since she's been seen," Ross pointed out.

"I know, Ross," Jenny replied in a soft voice. "Thanks for your offer, but I'm good."

Jenny stepped around the table and started to pass by Ross. She paused when he reached out a hand and touched her arm. Looking up, she could see the flash of regret in his eyes.

"Be careful," he finally said.

"Always," Jenny replied, pulling away.

She could feel Ross' gaze on her as she mumbled a thank you to Dorothy before pushing open the door and stepping out of the bar. Drawing in a deep breath of the salty air, she shoved her hands into her pockets.

The docks were empty now. The last of the fishermen were either visiting the pub or home with their families. Jenny wasn't ready to go back to the house where she and Carly used to live. The original owner had sold the house shortly after she'd moved out. The small cottage-style home was now available as a vacation rental. Renting that particular house might be a little morbid, but the new owners had completely remodeled the interior and exterior, and it felt like just a house instead of the home that she and Carly had created together.

Walking along the dimly lit dock, Jenny listened to the fading cries of a seagull and the occasional splash of a fish. The soothing sound of the water lapping against the dock and boats and the chill of the breeze drew the tension from her body.

She walked to the end of the dock and stopped. Pulling her hands out of her pockets, she gripped the railing and stared out at the fading light. Restless energy and grief made her feel on edge and uneasy.

"I have to move on with my life, Carly. Staying in Oregon isn't helping me do that. I thought moving away would, but I still feel like something is missing," Jenny murmured to the wind. She brushed the hair from her cheek and tucked it behind her ear. "Do you remember when we said we would go on a great adventure? You'd search the castles of Europe for dragons while I sailed the seven seas before we'd meet up to share our stories with each other." Jenny stood silently staring out at the horizon, lost in her memories of their childhood hopes and dreams. "After this week, I think it is time I took off for a while—maybe find a position overseas or on a cruise ship. There isn't anything here for me anymore. I miss you. Wherever you are, I hope we get to meet again one day."

Tears burned Jenny's eyes, but she blinked them away. She'd shed enough tears. Now it was time to embrace her belief that somehow, someway, Carly was safe and happy.

Jenny stepped back and pushed her hands into the pockets of her jacket. Her fingers closed around a small shell she had picked up along the trail earlier in the day. She tossed it over the railing, turned, and walked away. As she walked down the dock toward her car, she couldn't help but think that Carly was like the shell she had just tossed back into the ocean—a small, fragile treasure lost in a huge abyss.

CHAPTER THREE

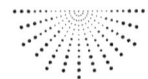

*L*ate the next afternoon, Jenny dejectedly walked down the trail back toward the parking lot. She reached the section where the path forked. The path ahead of her would lead her back to her car, the other went down to the beach.

Jenny bit her lip in indecision. She had always focused on the longest foot-trail. Carly had never been as enthusiastic about the water as Jenny had. Carly complained it was too cold, too rough, and contained things that liked to eat people. The memory of Carly's adamant refusal to go in the water during their high school years drew a soft chuckle from her.

Deciding the sound of the waves would help the depression she was feeling, she turned left and followed the uneven path through the thick woods and along the rocky cliff down to the beach. She paused near the edge of the rocks and looked out over the water. Once again, she'd discovered absolutely nothing on her trek today, but that wasn't a huge surprise. She would have been shocked if she had discovered something. Besides, she reasoned, not finding anything continued to give her hope that Carly was out there somewhere—alive and well.

Jenny thrust her hands into the back pockets of her jeans. Gazing out at the waves breaking against the rocky sand, she thought about her original plans to stay the entire week in Yachats. She'd planned to search for clues every day, but she was seriously considering calling it quits and driving back home later tonight.

After talking to Ross last night and her fruitless search today, she was thinking maybe it would be more productive to start researching her next move. If anything, the last two days had shown her that she was deluding herself into thinking she would find anything new. Ross was right; any evidence would have been destroyed over the past two years.

Jenny thought about her life. She didn't have anything to rush back to except an empty apartment. She was officially on summer break from the elementary school where she worked, and she had completed all the scheduled workshops. Now was the perfect time to start applying for positions elsewhere.

"It's hard to believe today marks exactly two years since you disappeared, Carly. I swear I don't know where time flies," Jenny said with a shake of her head.

She pulled her hands free from her pockets and reached up to unzip her jacket. She kicked at a few loose pebbles before stepping onto the loose sand. Walking toward the water, she breathed in the salty air.

The sound of the waves was already working its magic on her. She could feel the tension melting away. Her mind wandered as she glanced around. Instead of shelving the memories of Carly, she focused on the beautiful, cheerful girl who she had known since kindergarten. Flashes of their life together made her chuckle. Even though they weren't related by blood, they'd been as close as twins when it came to their silly pranks while growing up.

Jenny tucked her hands into her jacket pockets and scowled for a moment. If she ever found out who had hurt Carly, she would dice them into tiny cubes, pour soy sauce on the chopped up pieces, and stir fry their asses, then feed them to the fish. Yes, it sounded gross, but

Jenny didn't care. Anyone who could hurt someone as awesome as Carly deserved that and more.

She drew in a deep breath and focused on the small outcropping of rocks that rose out of the Pacific Northwest's cold ocean waters. Even with the unexpected sun streaming down, the air still held a distinct chill to it. A sad and reluctant smile curved Jenny's lips.

"You would totally hate this, Carly. You'd be ready to pack it in and head back home, call for a pizza delivery, and debate whether you should watch Dragonheart for the millionth time. God, I miss you and the way we could laugh together," Jenny murmured, staring out at the rocks.

A sense of peace washed through Jenny. In her own way, she'd said goodbye last night, and it was just sinking in now. It might not be closure, but it was as close to it as she could get. Releasing a deep breath, she turned to the left and started walking again down the beach when a brilliant sparkle brought her attention to the water's edge. Bending, she picked up an unusual stone half buried in the sand and seaweed. She straightened and gazed down at the colorful swirls embedded in the surface. Jenny rolled the smooth, cold stone in her hand, studying the vibrant lines running through it. Her fingers slowly tightened around the sea-polished gem that looked more like a priceless jewel than an unusual shell or piece of colorful sea glass. She turned her gaze back out toward the ocean.

Jenny closed her eyes and muttered a silent wish as she listened to the sounds of the waves, the birds, and the wind. She really did love the ocean; it was the one thing she missed the most besides Carly since her move to the suburbs of Portland.

She had spent just about every weekend coming here to swim, surf, hunt for shells and sea glass, or just to enjoy the sounds. Carly had thought she was nuts and suggested they move to some place like Florida or Hawaii, where at least the water was warmer, but Jenny didn't mind the cold. A dry suit and vigorous exercise were enough to keep her warm, even on a chilly day like today.

Jenny drew in a deep breath, enjoying the smell of the moist, chilly air as it coursed down into her lungs. A frown furrowed her brow when a child's laugh rose above the natural cadence of the waves and drew her out of her reverie.

Opening her eyes, she turned in time to see a shirtless young boy, around seven or eight, running toward the water not more than a dozen feet from where she was standing. She frowned when he didn't stop at the edge of it, but plowed forward into the rolling waves, heedless of the cold. She started forward in concern, scanning the beach for his parents or another adult, but the area was empty.

"Hey! Stop!" Jenny yelled. She shoved the rock she'd found in her front pants pocket before she took a step forward and held her hand out in warning. "Hey, you! Boy! Kid! Stop!"

The boy paused and glanced at her with wide, mischievous eyes before he grinned and dove under the next wave. Her summers as a lifeguard kicked in, and she kept her eyes glued on the tousled, white-blond head as she shrugged out of her jacket.

She let it fall to the ground behind her as she started running. Her tennis shoes would be a problem. She could kick them off once she hit the water. A part of her was concerned that her shirt and jeans would hinder her, but she didn't have time to strip out of them. The boy wasn't staying in the shallows, he was swimming straight out towards the horizon.

Her adrenaline spiked as she hit the freezing water. At the same time as the water closed around her thighs, she saw a flash of bright hair further ahead. The boy turned to look at her, amusement and an intense emotion she couldn't quite get a read on shining from his eyes. He smiled at her one more time before he slipped beneath the surface.

Jenny dove beneath the wave as it rolled over her. Kicking out with powerful strokes, she swept her arms out and cupped her hands to propel herself forward. She caught a glimpse of green when the sun broke through a cloud to shine down on the water. The boy had been wearing green pants. Hope built inside her as she swam harder than she ever had before. She ignored the burning in her lungs as long as she could, afraid that if she surfaced for air she would lose sight of the boy.

Frustration rose in her when the boy remained just out of reach. Unable to continue, Jenny rose to the surface and drew in a deep breath, the chilly air stinging her wet face. Panic began to sweep through her when she realized that the boy had not come up for air. She dove down, and swam in the direction where she had last seen him.

The water was deeper here, and Jenny could already feel the cold threatening to pull her down into the inky darkness. If not for the adrenaline and fear for the boy, she would have given up and returned to shore. Ignoring the stiffness in her limbs, she propelled herself downward. Her burning eyes caught sight of the boy a short distance in front of her. A sense of renewed determination filled her. She would NOT let him drown!

Just a little more, Jenny whispered to herself as she frantically kicked her legs. *You can do it.*

Jenny reached out, trying to grab the boy's foot. She didn't know how the kid could hold his breath so long or swim so fast. Her fingers skimmed the tips of his toes, startling him. She jerked her hand back when he suddenly turned and looked at her. Blinking, she paused when he pointed at a dark recess in a rocky formation. Her gaze involuntarily followed his arm in the direction he was pointing before darting back to him. A small stream of bubbles escaped past her lips when he motioned for her to follow him.

Shaking her head, she started to reach for him when he twisted away. A low cry of dismay resonated through her when she saw him disappear into the gap in the rock. Surging forward, she frantically grabbed at his foot again, missing it by less than a finger's width. Jenny gripped the rough edge of the rock and pulled herself forward until her head was just inside the narrow opening.

Her eyes widened when she saw a colorful kaleidoscope of water swirling in front of her. She barely caught a glimpse of the boy as he passed through it and disappeared. Unsure of what was going on, she gripped the rocky entrance to the cave with one hand while she reached out with the other to touch the colorful anomaly. The moment her fingers skimmed across the surface, she felt her body being pulled forward. A silent scream echoed in her mind as she was sucked forward into the whirlpool of colors.

CHAPTER FOUR

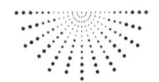

*J*enny's body twisted in the powerful rip current that held her. Her lungs burned with the need for oxygen, but she kept her lips firmly clamped shut. Even as her mind began to grow hazy, she fought to focus on finding the calm inside her.

One of her swim instructors had taught her that meditating helped in situations like this by reducing your heart rate and decreasing the need for oxygen. Jenny had practiced the method and increased her underwater time to almost three and a half minutes, but that was in a pool. Her body bounced off of the edge of a rock, and she winced. Her blurry vision was darkening, and she knew she was seconds away from drowning.

Reaching out, Jenny tried to grab the rocky side of the cavern. She was surprised when a small hand wrapped around her wrist. Jenny found herself being dragged forward at an incredible speed. Blinking, she saw a faint light up above her.

Suddenly, she began to rise upward. Jenny fought against the fuzzy darkness and kicked her feet in an effort to help the boy pull her up. Her lips parted against her will as the last bit of oxygen in her lungs coursed through her body. Panic changed to relief when they surfaced into a dim cavern.

Jenny gulped desperately needed air into her starving lungs. She briefly caught sight of another small boy sitting on a ledge before the boy holding her wrist started pulling her toward the sandy shore. The movement caused her to slip under the water for a brief second while her mouth was still open, making her gag on a mouthful of water. Fighting to rise to the surface again, she spat out the water and fought the urge to cough.

She forced her shivering body to respond to her demands even as exhaustion threatened to drag her down. If she gave in now, she would sink below the surface and drown. Forcing her legs to move, she clumsily frog-kicked to the edge of the pool.

"Just a little farther," the boy's soft voice echoed in the cave.

Jenny clenched her jaw to keep her teeth from chattering. She felt frozen to the bone. She tried to grasp the edge of the pool but couldn't get her fingers to work. Two sets of small hands pulled on her trembling arms, dragging her out of the water.

Jenny collapsed onto the hard surface and rolled onto her back. As she stared up at the twinkling green lights of the cavern ceiling, several things registered through her mind even as darkness began to spread. The most important was, where in the hell was she? Too tired to contemplate the answer, Jenny felt her body relax as the warmth of the cave surrounded her chilled, exhausted body. Her eyelids fluttered briefly when she heard the sound of voices, but she was beyond dealing with it at the moment. The last of her resistance dissolved, and she slipped into semi-consciousness.

∾

"What is she?" the younger child's voice asked as a small hand touched the highlights in Jenny's auburn-colored hair. "Her hair looks like the fire coral mixed with the sun."

"She's ours is what she is," a voice whispered. "I captured her for us."

"Father–"

"I don't care what he says. Time is running out. You heard what Kelia and the other servants were saying. If Father does not find a wife soon, the kingdom will be in trouble. We should have some say in who will be our mother. The Goddess said so," the older boy said stubbornly.

"I know, but the Sea Witch…. She scares me, Dolph," the young boy said.

Dolph waved his hand in the air. "She was the only one who could help us. This is the one, Juno. I can feel it. She is ours. The Sea Witch promised if I found a woman with hair the color of our fire coral caught in the sun and brought her back, she would be ours."

"But… What if she doesn't want to be ours?" Juno asked.

Jenny decided she'd remained silent long enough when she heard the tremble in the younger boy's voice. Her brain had finally kicked into gear a minute ago as the last of the freezing cold numbness melted away. Her body had remained relaxed as she listened to the two boys' conversation, even when she'd felt the touch of small fingers on her hair. The gentle, soothing strokes told her that she wasn't in any danger. She'd lain there trying to establish in her mind what had happened.

She replayed the entire incident from the moment she'd seen the boy with the white hair run past her to the second she slipped into semi-consciousness. Nothing made sense to her. Rolling over onto her side, she bit back a groan of pain from the movement.

The gentle lapping of waves pulled her gaze to the ground. She was lying on a long, narrow stretch of shimmering pink sand. Once again, she remembered the pairs of small hands tugging her exhausted body up onto what turned out to be a small beach inside a cave.

Confusion washed over her, and she curled her fingers in the warm sand. Because it felt so good against her chilled skin, a part of her wished she could burrow down into the silky granules like one of the coquinas she used to play with on the beach when her parents visited Florida. Releasing the powdery particles, she turned her head to look at the boy she had followed here.

"Where…," she started to say before she cleared her raw throat. "Where am I?"

Her voice was hoarse from the salt water she had swallowed. She struggled to sit up when she heard the sounds of the boys scooting quickly backwards. Pushing her shoulder-length hair out of her face, she blinked several times to clear her vision.

"Where am I?" she demanded again in a thick voice before it faded in stunned disbelief as she got her first good look around the vast cavern where she found herself. "Oh! Wow!"

She stared up at the ceiling in amazement. It was stone, but it was glittering like a million stars that were captured in a huge net. Her eyes ran down the wall, stopping at a shallow ledge on the far side where a dozen small creatures with dark green scales and large black eyes stared back at her. The species looked like a cross between a seahorse and a frog. Several of the creatures jumped off the narrow shelf and disappeared beneath the water. Turning her head, she stared into the vivid green eyes of the older boy she'd seen back on the beach.

"Where in the *hel*– heck am I?" Jenny growled in a low voice filled with unease. "What are those things?"

The boy stood up. She studied him more closely for the first time. His hair was white-blond and cut short. His eyes were a bright, vivid green with specks of forest green. She had never seen such a beautiful shade of green before. She slowly ran her gaze over him. He had put on a brown shirt that hung down over his dark green pants, both made of some kind of fabric that she had never seen before. The clothes looked as if they might be water proof. His feet were still bare. He had long toes that curled in the sand when she gazed at them.

Was that webbing between them? she wondered as she returned her gaze to his thin face.

"They are young sea dragons," the boy replied. "You are on the Isle of the Sea Serpent."

The boy's voice was polite, but there was also a hint of determination in it that far exceeded his age. She could tell by the way his jaw was thrust forward that he was used to getting his own way. Personally, she didn't give a damn. She dealt with twenty-four third graders in one of the toughest schools in Portland. Raising an eyebrow, she stared back at him in silence.

It took a few seconds longer than it normally did, but she saw a shadow of doubt come into his eyes, and he glanced at the boy next to him. Jenny waited as they engaged in a silent argument. Finally, the second boy shook his head and shifted uneasily in the sand.

"We are going to be in so much trouble this time," the boy muttered, glancing at Jenny again. "So very much trouble when Father finds out what we have done."

Jenny couldn't quite stop the reluctant smile that tugged at her lips. The younger boy looked so despondent that she couldn't help but feel sorry for him. He was several years younger than the boy from the beach, but he had the same white-blond hair and piercing green eyes. Jenny shook her head and released a deep sigh as she shifted until she was sitting cross-legged. She reached down and cupped a handful of the pink sand in her left hand. Tilting her hand, she watched as the granules flowed back down to the ground to form a small, sparkling pile.

"Isle of the Sea Serpent, huh?" she asked, looking up at the boys with a crooked smile. "Do you boys have names?" she continued when they both gave her a sharp nod.

The younger boy's smile was hopeful, and he glanced at his older brother. The older one stepped forward and bent at the waist in a stiff bow before straightening. He gave her a mischievous smile before answering her. Jenny couldn't help but be enchanted by his debonair behavior.

"I am Dolph," the boy said in a voice that belied his age. "And this is my brother, Juno."

Jenny's lips twitched when the other boy imitated Dolph. "I'm Jenny," she replied, glancing back and forth between them. "I'm not sure what happened, but something tells me I'm really not supposed to be here, am I?"

A flash of guilt crossed the boys' faces. Their expressions were enough to answer her question. They both had a pensive look mixed with unease, hope, and determination. She'd also heard enough of their earlier conversation to realize that there was some important information that she needed to understand everything that was happening.

"No," Juno muttered before he grinned. "But, I'm glad you are. How did you get hair the color of the fire coral? Did the Sea Witch cast a spell on you? When I touched it, it did not burn me. How can that be?"

Jenny reached up and touched her hair. "I was born with red hair. Haven't you ever seen anyone with red hair before?" she asked, shifting so she could stand up.

A wrinkle of surprise creased her brow when she noticed that instead of being sandy like she normally was after a visit to the beach, the pink crystals fell away from her damp clothes. She shivered and wrapped her arms around her waist. Her gaze locked on the young sea dragons on the far side of the cave.

"Is there an adult nearby? Someone who knows where you are?" Jenny asked, turning back to look at the two boys.

"Of course! We have a nursemaid. She will eventually catch up with us," Juno assured her with a grin.

Jenny smiled wryly at that and shook her head at Juno's happy, innocent expression. She couldn't leave them unsupervised.

"Listen, I need to get back home. Before I do that, we should find your nursemaid," she said in a firm tone.

"But... You can't go back!" Juno exclaimed with a vigorous shake of his head. He stepped forward and grabbed her hand as if to make sure she didn't suddenly disappear. "Dolph said you would help us."

When she heard the note of panic in his voice, Jenny knelt down and gently squeezed Juno's small hand in reassurance. "Why can't I go back? Are you in danger? Has someone hurt you or your brother? If you need help, I can contact the authorities. I heard you say your father would be upset. If he has hurt you, that isn't right," Jenny explained.

"Father would never hurt us," Juno replied, "He gets exas… exasgurated because our nursemaid loses us," Juno glanced at his brother with a wry smile before turning to gaze at Jenny again. "But he never gets angry. He just says he has to find a nursemaid who is smarter than we are."

Jenny chuckled. "Then what is it?"

Juno looked down and tears glittered in his eyes for a moment before he furiously blinked them back. Jenny turned to look up at Dolph who was staring back at her with that same determined look he had before.

"Dolph, what is going on?" Jenny asked in a calm voice. Something in his eyes suddenly made her feel just how small they were within the vast cavern, and her gut instinct told her she really wasn't going to like what she was about to hear. She dropped her left hand and carefully pinched her leg to see if she was really awake. The sharp sting told her that she was. This was definitely not a dream.

"Dolph! Juno!" a woman's voice called frantically in the distance.

Jenny turned to look toward the sound. It took her a moment to notice the shadowed opening in one recess of the cavern. She almost fell forward when she felt Juno pulling anxiously on her hand. She stood, still grasping his hand.

"Who is that?" she asked.

"Kelia," Dolph replied, looking apprehensively at the entrance to the cavern.

"Dolph, Juno!"

Jenny could hear the exasperation in the woman's voice. It looked like the boys were going to need a new, smarter-than-them nanny soon. She jerked forward when Juno pulled on her hand.

She cast a quick glance at the large pool of water behind her. The sea dragons were crawling up the far wall again and settling back on the dozens of narrow ledges. For a brief second, Jenny could have sworn they were watching her with gleeful eyes. Unable to resist, she stuck her tongue out at them before turning back to watch where she was going.

If someone had told her this morning that she would be taking a fantastic and bizarre journey to a mystical world, she would never have believed them. She stumbled when it suddenly dawned on her that maybe Carly wasn't killed by a serial killer like the police thought after all. Maybe, just maybe, she had been swept away here. Carly had been in the park when she disappeared. If it was possible for Jenny to find a way to a different world, perhaps Carly had too.

"Dolph," Jenny called, hurrying after the older boy.

Dolph paused and turned at the entrance to the cavern to look back at her. Once again, she saw an expression in the young boy's eyes that spoke of a maturity that was unusual in someone so young. He gazed at her in silence.

"Did another woman…? Do you know or have you heard of another woman like me, only with brown hair, that might have come here? She would have been about this tall, with brown eyes. She… It would have been a couple of years ago," Jenny asked, holding her left hand up in the air to show how tall Carly was.

Dolph shook his head. "No. We would have heard if there had been another from your world. The Sea Witch helped me create the portal to bring you through. The water told me where I had to open it," he replied with a shake of his head.

"Oh," Jenny said, disappointed. "Well, perhaps someone else may have heard something."

She wasn't quite ready to give up. If there was one way into this place, there might be another. Perhaps one of the adults had heard something. It couldn't hurt to ask around, maybe do a little exploring. Honestly, what did she have to lose?

Excitement began to build inside her the more she thought about it. She was in another world—or at least she was pretty sure she was from the little she had seen so far. Those creatures back in the cave didn't look or move like any animatronics she had ever seen. Besides, it wasn't like there were any pressing reasons for her to rush back. As long as she could find her way back to the cavern, she had a way home. She had hoped for a change in her life, maybe this was her chance.

CHAPTER FIVE

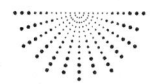

Dolph led the way out of the cavern along a narrow, winding path. The pink sand gave way to stones worn smooth over time. Each stone contained more of the green lights, creating enough ambient glow to light their way. Jenny had to resist the urge to stop and touch the specks of light. As they walked, she could see more of them reflecting off the rough, rocky walls all the way to the entrance. The dark gray walls curved to the left, blocking her view of what was beyond until she stepped completely out of the cave.

Jenny jerked to a stop and blinked when they emerged into a lush, thick garden. She had expected the cave to open out onto a beach. Her eyes swept over the brilliantly colored plants that looked more like the coral found along the Great Barrier Reef than something you'd find in a garden above the sea. Heck, some of the vibrant plants even moved like the sea anemones she had seen in fish tanks and on television. Her eyes followed one stunning orange, red, and purple plant that rose up toward the….

"Oh, my!" she whispered, staring up at the large, crystal clear dome that created a ceiling. Sunlight filtered through the lavender colored water on the other side of the dome. Large fish, some the size of a blue whale, swam overhead. "This is unbelievable. I really am in another world!"

"Dolph, Juno, where have you two been?! I've been looking all over for y... ou." Kelia's voice faded as she stared at Jenny in stunned disbelief. "Oh my! What have you two done now? Oh, Dolph, your father will. ..."

Pulling her gaze away from Kelia's shocked face when a shadow passed overhead, Jenny looked back up at the dome as a group of large sea dragons swam past. Her loud hiss echoed through the air when she saw the riders on the creatures' backs.

"What in the hell is this place?" Jenny whispered in awe.

~

Orion swung the staff in his hand and fired a burst of energy from it. The force of the powerful charge hit the twenty foot Megatooth shark in the side, forcing it to veer off to the left and disappear into the murky darkness. Adjusting his grip on the power rod in his hand, he kept a wary eye on the beast to make sure it didn't reappear. His other arm was wrapped tightly around the limp body of a warrior who had been injured during their mission. With a growl of frustration, he turned and watched as a group of his men appeared out of the deep purple abyss not far from where he had originally emerged with the wounded warrior.

"Your Majesty," his Captain of the Guard called as he drew near. "We have been successful in our quest," Kapian added, holding up a cloth bag before his gaze shifted to the unconscious warrior in Orion's arms. "How bad is Cyrus?"

Orion swung his leg over the back of his stag when the large sea dragon drew close. "He will live," he replied, pulling back on the reins as he settled Cyrus across his thighs. "He needs medical attention, though. The shark took us by surprise."

"Why would shark be in this region?" Kapian asked with a frown. "The beasts normally do not come up from the depths or this far east."

"I suspect the Sea Witch enchanted the creature to protect her lair," Orion replied with a shrug as he surged forward, heading back to the Isle of the Sea Serpent. "My cousin has become too bold. I will have to deal with her once and for all. I had hoped…." Orion's voice faded and he shook his head.

Kapian pulled his light yellow and orange stag up beside Orion's. "She knows the end of your allotted grieving period draws near. Juno's fifth year of birth is just a few days away. If you have not taken another bride by that time, she will challenge the law and press her claim to the throne regardless of what she has done. You must choose another bride soon. If Magna is successful with her claim, she will take control and declare war on the remaining kingdoms. You saw the resulting devastation her power caused to the Isle of the Dragons."

"I know, Kapian!" Orion retorted sharply before he lowered his voice. "You think me blind to the frozen bodies of the dragons she turned to stone? Every realm felt the moment Drago went silent. The visages of his people lying scattered across the ocean floor are a constant reminder of my failure to stop my cousin. If I had the power to reverse the spell I would, but the danger is too great to tamper with unknown spells. If I failed, I could destroy them all. I leave them there as a reminder of the danger Magna represents to all the kingdoms, not just the Isle of the Sea Serpent, and with the hope that one day the spell can be reversed. Without the full power of the trident, the threat is even greater."

"I know you wish to capture Magna alive in the hopes of forcing her to undo her unnatural magic, but you may have to concede that you will never be able to do so. We have recovered one of the Eyes of the Sea Serpent she stole from you. We can now retrieve the other one. In the meantime, you must choose another bride to secure the kingdom's future now. There is no longer any time to delay," Kapian pressed.

Orion shot Kapian an impatient look, but didn't reply. Instead, he pressed his knees against the side of his stag and pulled ahead of his

Captain of the Guard. He knew what was at stake; he didn't need Kapian's constant reminders or his friend's suggestions as to who he should choose as his bride. His first bride had been chosen for him by his parents. Shamill's death during the birth of their youngest son, Juno, had been unfortunate. He had no desire to have another bride chosen for him.

Orion silently admitted that he had hoped that with two sons, he would be immune to the need for a bride, but as powerful as he was, this law he could not change. His people believed that to have balance, a King needed a Queen by his side. He also knew that both of his sons wished to have a mother instead of the series of nursemaids he had employed.

So far, he had resisted everyone's demands, even the ones made by Magna. He shuddered as he thought of his cousin's unexpected appearance nearly a week ago and her attempt to pressure him to take her as his mate. The beautiful, mischievous girl he had known in his youth had changed into someone he didn't recognize.

She had appeared in his dreams at first. The sound of her voice, softly calling to him, beckoning him to come to her, help her, and give in to her pleas. At first, her physical appearance reminded him of the days before the war until he saw the glow in her eyes. Gone was the soft innocence. Her eyes had swirled with a malevolent blackness that reminded him of the tar pits found on one of the small, outer islands.

Sensing danger, he had jerked awake to realize that it was not a dream. Magna had somehow slipped past the wards he had cast and invaded the inner sanctuary of his living quarters. Surging out of his bed, he had wrapped his hands around her arms to capture her.

"What are…?" Orion hissed when she didn't resist.

"Help me, Orion. I can't fight it any longer," Magna whispered, staring back at him with haunted eyes for a moment before her face contorted in pain. "Dragon's fire and… the… trident. Don't let him get the trident…."

Orion's eyes widened when wisps of black vapor began to rise from

Magna's skin and solidify. He suddenly found his body rising off the floor before being flung back against the wall by ghost-like hands coiled in a powerful black essence. Catching himself as he started to slide down the wall, he watched Magna's expression transform into something he no longer recognized.

"Join with me, Orion. Accept me as your bride, and you will have all the power of the universe at your disposal," Magna had whispered.

"I don't want or need the power of the universe. Magna. I will also never join with you. You know our laws demand balance. Your greed for power is too great for that ever to happen," Orion retorted.

Magna's eyes glowed with an eerie, unnatural light. "Give me the trident, Orion. With my powers, we could rule the Seven Kingdoms," she said.

"The power held in the trident is not to be abused," Orion replied, taking a step forward and pulling on his own magical abilities. "Whatever happened to you, Magna, you are no longer the girl I remember. She would never have harmed another. You brought laughter and love to the world. Now, you bring death and destruction."

The dark essence swirling around her began to fade as he spoke. He took a step closer to her and raised his hand in a silent invitation. A sixth sense told him that if he tried to cast the spell now, whatever was swirling around her would protect her. The only way to ensure the spell he was forming would work would be if he could touch her.

"Orion...?"

For a moment, a glimpse of the young girl he'd known appeared in her eyes again. Fear, resignation, and despair warred within the dark brown depths. Her gaunt features showed that whatever was inside her was slowly destroying her. He didn't know what the thing could be, but in that moment he understood that she was battling the darkness that was wrapped around her like the arms of an octopus.

"Give yourself up to me, Magna. I will do what I can to help you," Orion gently encouraged.

"He won't let me," she replied in a weary voice, bowing her head.

"Who won't? You speak as if there are two of you," Orion said.

Magna's head rose and her expression changed. Her eyes grew hard and distant again, and the black bands struck out at him. Orion called for the trident. His hands wrapped around it as long, black tentacles shot out.

Orion was shocked when the tentacles reached for the jewel-encrusted staff, absorbing the power sparking from the prongs of trident instead of falling away from the intense energy it was emitting. A curse exploded from Orion's lips when his efforts to send the trident away were blocked. He could hear Magna's voice rising as she cast the spell to stop him.

Gripping the trident near the top with one hand, he tried to reach out and touch Magna with his other. Orion felt his body rising off the floor again. He jerked his hand back and wound it around the carved golden staff in an attempt to hold onto it. Whatever magic Magna was using, it felt as if it were alive. Small, greedy fingers curled into sharp talons. It took a moment to realize that they were clawing at the Eyes of the Sea Serpent embedded in the trident.

Orion watched in disbelief when one of the gems loosened under the continued attack. He shot out his hand and captured the falling jewel before she could. A ferocious snarl of rage escaped Magna.

Orion turned his head toward his cousin when he felt her release her grip on the trident. Her hands rose to claw at his face. He stumbled backwards away from her, but didn't have time to escape her next attack. A large mass of the black swirling cloud coalesced and burst out toward him.

Raising the trident to help protect himself, the mass still hit him with enough ferocity that he was flung off his feet. The second wave lifted his body up and tossed him out of the open doors to the balcony. Orion slammed into the floor and slid across the balcony.

A hiss escaped Orion when he realized that the railing was gone.

Grasping the trident with one hand, he dug it into the floor of the balcony, the prongs screeched loudly as they gouged long grooves in the stone. He stopped on the edge with his feet hanging over.

Using the trident, he pulled himself up onto the balcony and rose to his feet. His gaze glittered with anger and determination. He stepped away from the gap in the railing. Swinging his gaze around to his cousin, Orion was stunned by the transformation in her.

Her body floated a few inches from the ground. The black essence that had attacked him radiated from her skin like sea snakes. Her hair floated as if caught in a rip current under the sea.

Whatever magic Magna awakened, it is growing more powerful, he thought as his fingers closed around the gem in his hand.

"Give me the Eye of the Sea Serpent, Orion," Magna ordered, stepping out onto the balcony.

"That will never happen," Orion retorted, holding the trident in one hand and the gem in the other.

"I gave you the chance to join with me! The Isle of the Sea Serpent could be the most powerful kingdom of all. Now I will take the kingdom and the power of the trident from you!" Magna snarled, lifting her hands.

This time, Orion was prepared. He raised the trident and shouted a command to the water far below to rise. A high pressure stream collided with the swirling black bands. For a brief moment, whatever dark magic Magna was using fought against the powerful pressure.

Orion wasn't prepared for the other bands that snaked out and sliced through the water. He barely had time to dive to the side when they shot forward like deadly spears determined to pierce his body. Rolling as he landed on the hard floor, the hand holding the loose gem opened and the gem tumbled across the balcony.

Magna rushed toward the gem, her hand reaching for it even as Orion pushed to his feet in an effort to stop her. His hand closed around her slender wrist. For a moment, they wrestled with each other, the dark bands striking at him with a ferocity that left long welts along his arms, chest, and face.

In fury, Orion drew upon the power of the sea to come to his aid yet again. A large wave flowed around him and struck Magna, lifting her up. Her fingers lost their grip on the gem and it slipped away in the rushing water. Again, his gaze locked with hers and for a brief moment the young girl had returned. Regret and sadness glistened in her eyes before she closed them and she suddenly faded away.

Orion stood on the balcony breathing heavily, stunned by the encounter. He gripped the trident in his hand and stepped over to the railing to look down. His cousin was gone.

At least he had the trident. He would command the sea to return the Eye of the Sea Serpent that had been swept away. Straightening, he turned the trident in his hand. The command on his lips died and fury swelled inside him when he saw not one, but two empty eye sockets on the winding serpent molded into the trident.

"Magna!" Orion roared when he realized what his cousin had done, turning to look down at the swirling dark water far below.

∾

Orion dragged his mind back to the present. He knew the only thing standing between the safety of his people and the devastation Magna could create was the power he wielded as the rightful king of the sea people. Without both gems, the trident's power to control the oceans would be limited. The trident contained its own power, but without the gift from the Goddess, there would be an imbalance in the world. He had ordered the sea to return the gem that had been swept away, but his requests had not been answered.

It also didn't help that his encounter with Magna had increased the pressure on him to find a bride. Frustration built up inside him as the weight of his responsibilities threatened to crush him. He had no doubt that Magna would try to prevent him from finding another wife now that she realized he would never willingly choose her.

He would just have to ask the first maiden he came across when he returned. His mind flitted through the few unattached women in the palace and he came up with a blank. Every woman he could think of was already married. He wondered if he had subconsciously ordered Kelia only to employ married or attached women in an effort to distance himself from having to make a choice.

The problem was the emptiness he felt deep inside. None of the women who had come forth over the last few years had aroused his curiosity, much less desire in his loins. Only Dolph and Juno's presence kept the dark void of loneliness at bay.

Orion reined Sea Fire through the long, clear tunnel leading into the underwater city. The city of the Isle of the Sea Serpent was unique because it existed both below the water and above. The isle rose up out of the ocean with steep, treacherous cliffs circling the majority of the island. Sharp, jagged rocks formed by the island's long extinct volcanoes stood as deadly barricades against attacks.

Even if an enemy could penetrate this barrier, the steep walls of the cliffs were impossible to scale. The only safe entries were through narrow passages that were well guarded from above and below the sea. More than a dozen smaller, uninhabited islands formed a chain off the coast and were preserved for the abundant wildlife that made their home along the reefs around the Isle of the Sea Serpent.

Sea Fire broke through the shields holding back the water from the underground city, settling on his four webbed feet once he was on the entry platform. Orion handed Cyrus off to a group of medics before climbing off his stag. Handing the reins to an attendant, he wondered where Dolph and Juno were. They were usually close by, eagerly waiting on his return so he could tell them of his adventures. Just the thought of their excited, inquisitive faces lifted the corner of his lips in a smile of amusement.

Turning to gaze around him with a frown, Orion looked for his old nursemaid who normally kept an eye on the boys. She was the only nursemaid they would listen to now. He had dismissed almost a dozen others after finding they could not control the two boys.

His gaze locked on Kelia as she pushed through the crowd. The worried expression on the older woman's face did not bode well for her willingness to continue to assist him going forth. He feared her advanced age was catching up with her and she was getting exasperated with Dolph and Juno's constant antics.

"What did they do this time? Have they disappeared again?" he asked in a gruff voice as he walked toward her.

Kelia gave him a reassuring smile, even as she shook her head. "They are at the palace," she replied with a hesitant smile. She glanced at the other men who were still entering the city. "I do need to speak with you about a possible… cause for concern that may have arisen while you were gone, Your Majesty."

Orion gave Kelia a suspicious glance before nodding. Waving his hand for her to walk beside him, he glowered when she took a slight step to the left and behind him. Old habits die hard. He released a tired sigh when Kapian called out to him.

"Your Majesty," Kapian said with a short bow before he held out his hand. "The item you requested."

Orion's mouth tightened at his forgetfulness. Reaching out his right hand, he took the light brown bag from Kapian. He quickly tugged at the bindings holding it closed and looked inside. Satisfied with the contents, he gave Kapian a piercing look to remind him to keep what was found a secret.

"Debrief the others and meet with me later this evening," Orion ordered, turning back toward the palace. "Kelia, tell me what mischief my sons have been in while I was away. I assume they are the reason behind this sudden concern. I fear they may have given you a challenging day."

"More than usual, Your Majesty," Kelia informed him with a hint of worry and a touch of amusement. "They have outdone themselves this time."

Orion shook his head. "I find that hard to believe," he muttered with a shake of his head as he climbed the steps leading up to the entrance.

"This time is different, Your Majesty," Kelia replied in a quiet, serious voice as she stared up into his vivid, dark green eyes.

"What is it?" Orion asked, drawing in a deep breath as the sinking feeling in his stomach grew.

"They have found a mother for themselves," Kelia informed him with a smile. "She is unlike anyone I have seen before."

CHAPTER SIX

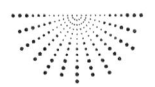

Fury warred with disbelief. What was his oldest son thinking?! The pool of the Sea Dragon was a forbidden area. For as long as Orion could remember—hell, for as long as the Isle of the Sea Serpent had existed—the magical pool had been off-limits. It was said that only the young sea dragons went to the cavern to play. No one knew how the sea dragons made it into the magical pool or out of it. As children, Orion, Magna, and Kapian had spent hours searching for the underwater entrance. They had even dared to sneak into the cavern late one night.

A shiver of unease ran through him at the remembrance of that night. They had been young and stupid. If not for the sudden appearance of his father, they could have been swept to another world and never found their way back.

Years later, Orion read in a document in the ancient archives that the pool contained a portal to the realm where the waters of two worlds mixed. He couldn't help but believe it after his own experience. If Dolph went through the portal, he might never have been able to find his way back home. The fact that Juno had been in the cavern as well shook him to the core. The thought of losing both of his sons at the same time made Orion's stomach clench with fear.

His long legs ate up the distance, bringing him down the corridor to the suite of rooms he shared with the two boys. The closer he got, the more furious he became. This time the boys had gone too far. Not only had they endangered their own lives, but they had possibly endangered the life of someone from another realm. If Dolph had somehow whisked a maiden from another kingdom to the Isle of the Sea Serpent without her permission, it could be taken as an act of war.

The two older warriors standing outside his rooms recognized his furious expression and gave him a swift look of empathy before the one on the left reached out and grasped the door handle to pull the door open. Orion slowed almost to a stop and drew in a deep breath. He glanced at the warrior holding the door open.

"The young princes' care only for you and the kingdom, Your Majesty," Coralus said with a shake of his head. "You have to give them some credit for their tenacity."

The comment did little to calm Orion. With a grimace, he shook his head at Kelia's spouse. Coralus was all too familiar with the trials and tribulations of being a parent—and the numerous stories of his sons' adventures.

"Dolph!" Orion loudly called as he strode through the door and into his living quarters. "Are you out of your mind, boy?! Kelia said that you have found a...."

Orion stumbled to a stop, frozen in mid-stride, and swallowed when a delicate face lifted to gaze up at him. A cascade of red hair with the stunning hues of hot flowing lava fell around the woman's bemused face. From her expression, she looked as if she were caught in a trap she didn't know how to escape. His eyes slowly tore away from hers. He was unsure of their color, but it reminded him of sea glass in a variety of colors. He vaguely noted the faint trace of dots across her nose before his gaze fastened on her parted lips.

A surge of need, unlike anything he had felt before, struck him hard and fast. His physical response was so strong and so unexpected that he took several steps forward before he realized what he was doing. Orion clenched his fists at his side, his left hand clutching the bag Kapian had given him in an effort to keep from grabbing the woman as she pushed up off the floor where she had been playing a game with Juno.

"Who...? Where...?" he mumbled incoherently before he stopped and drew in a deep breath. He shook his head and straightened his shoulders. "Who are you, and where did you come from?" he demanded in a terse tone.

He silently moaned when the woman tilted her head and looked at him with a raised eyebrow. He swore he could feel the heat inside him increase into a full blown inferno, much like the fire of the dragons. He released a low growl of frustration at the thought of comparing anything to the snarly beasts that lived on the Isle of the Dragons. The sound of his son's voice refocused his attention on the situation instead of his physical reaction to the woman standing in front of him.

"Father," Dolph said, coming to stand between the woman and his father.

"Go tell Coralus to take you and your brother to Kelia," Orion ordered in a stern voice, not looking at his oldest son.

"Father...," Dolph protested.

Orion glanced at his oldest son with a stern expression. "Now, Dolph. I will speak with you later."

"But, Father," Juno protested, standing to hold onto Jenny's hand. "She's ours. She can be our new mother. She likes to play games with me."

Orion's face softened at the pleading expression in his youngest son's eyes. Where Dolph had found such a beautiful woman, he had no idea. The one thing he did know was that she was not from the Isle of the Sea Serpents.

"Go with your brother, Juno," Orion gently commanded. "Kelia is waiting for you both."

Juno reluctantly released the hand he was clutching and bowed his head as he followed Dolph out of the room. Orion turned to watch the boys as they paused in the entrance to the door that still stood open. His eyes locked with Dolph's suddenly stony expression.

"She's the one, Father," Dolph said stubbornly. "I know she is. The water led me to her."

Orion watched in silence as the boys left, closing the door quietly behind them. Drawing in a deep breath, he turned to face the woman. She was watching him with a look of sympathy and bemusement. He raised his right hand and ran it over the back of his neck.

"Who are you and which kingdom did you come from so I can make sure you are safely returned?" he demanded in a gruff voice as he dropped his hand back to his side.

∽

Jenny fingered the soft material of the long, forest green blouse as she slid it on over a pair of dark tan trousers. Kelia had escorted her through the magical garden to a magnificent castle. The older woman had spoken in a soft voice to several other women as they entered. Jenny missed most of what Kelia had said because she couldn't stop staring up at the clear dome and the colorful fish that passed overhead. She finally guessed what the discussion was about when one of the women appeared with fresh clothing a short time after they arrived at the elegant but inviting suite of rooms.

They had no sooner entered the large, elegantly furnished room before Kelia led Jenny to an exquisite bathroom to freshen up. The older woman bowed and explained that she would have refreshments available in the living room when Jenny was finished. It didn't take long for Jenny to figure out how to work the plumbing. She softly groaned as the warm water took the last of the chill from her bones and washed the salt from her hair and body. Twenty minutes later, she felt refreshed and excited to explore this new, fascinating world she now found herself in.

Jenny retraced the path to the living room. She paused at the entrance and quietly watched Kelia and another woman place several small trays on a side table. She smiled when Kelia teasingly scolded Juno for pinching one of the pastries.

"But, I had to grab it. It was about to fall and you always told me that if I touch a piece of food, I needed to eat it," Juno defended around a mouthful of the flaky bun.

"It is amazing how often food, especially your favorite, always falls off of the tray and into your mouth at just the right moment," Kelia chuckled.

"This one looks wobbly, too," Dolph said, snatching not one, but two pastries before he danced out of Kelia's reach with a laugh.

"I'll admit, the one with the purple filling did look like it might fall off," Jenny teased with a wink at Dolph.

Dolph grinned in delight at having her support. Jenny decided it wouldn't hurt to support the little boy. She figured he was probably starving after his adventure earlier. She knew she was.

"Those look delicious," Jenny said, walking over to where Kelia was standing.

"The chef is known for his pastries. They melt in your mouth and stay on your hips," Kelia chuckled, running her hands down her sides.

"Well, one can't hurt too much," Jenny laughed.

She picked up one of the pastries with a dark red filling and took a bite. A soft moan of pleasure escaped her when the flaky dough melted in her mouth. The filling was still warm and the sweet taste of the fruit washed over her taste buds.

"The problem is stopping at just one," Kelia said, picking up one of the cream filled delicacies with a rueful look.

Jenny covered her mouth and giggled. Kelia was right, there was no way she would be able to resist trying another one… or two. Picking up a bun with a mixture of nuts on it, she walked over to the window to gaze out over the gardens before glancing up at the crystal dome again. Her hand lowered and she stared in awe. Several large whales were pulling carts behind them. They passed overhead before disappearing from view.

"This world is… incredible," Jenny whispered.

"I hope you find it fascinating enough to want to stay, Lady Jenny," Kelia replied.

A smile pulled at Jenny's lips and she dragged her gaze away from the crystal dome to stare down at the colorful garden with its bizarre yet beautiful plants. Her head turned when she felt a small hand slide into hers. Her gaze softened when she saw the hopeful expression on Juno's face.

"I hope you do stay, Jenny, and be our mother," Juno replied.

Jenny's throat tightened at the earnest tone and slightly pleading look in the little boy's gaze. How could she extinguish that look from his eyes? She squeezed his hand and turned to look at Dolph. The older boy was studying her with a quiet, determined gaze.

"Why don't you tell me about your home," Jenny replied lightly.

Nearly three hours later, Jenny had more questions than when she'd first arrived. According to Kelia and the boys, she was in a magical underwater kingdom ruled by the Sea King. The Isle of the Sea Serpent belonged to the sea people, aka mermaids and mermen. Dolph and Juno had burst out laughing when Jenny called them mermaids and had teased her endlessly about it.

For the last hour, Jenny had played games with the boys while Kelia ran an errand. Jenny hadn't minded. The two boys were delightful and extremely well behaved. After Dolph found some colorful rocks and shells along with some twine, she showed the boys how to create a Tic-Tac-Toe board with the materials. She had been coaching Juno on how to move his pieces when the door burst open and a very sexy but furious man suddenly stormed in.

It took less than five seconds to figure out that this was the boys' father. She would have been intimidated by the six feet plus of muscled fury if she hadn't noticed the blatant look of shock on his face when he saw her or the way his expression softened when he gazed at Dolph.

She practically melted when he turned his gaze on Juno after the young boy protested. The expression in his eyes showed that this was a man who knew how to love and wasn't afraid to show it. Jenny felt the tug on her heartstrings and knew she was doomed. This was a man who could take her heart prisoner any time he wanted as far as she was concerned.

Needless to say, the whole encounter shook her. She had never been a believer of attraction at first sight. Now she would have to re-evaluate the possibility. Of course, she was still trying to come to terms with the fact that she wasn't on Earth—or at least not on a part of it that she had ever heard about before. Jenny flushed when she noticed that she had been so focused on the man in front of her that the boys had left the room before she realized it, leaving her alone with their father.

"Who are you and which kingdom did you come from?" he asked again.

"I was from Yachats, Oregon, but I moved to Portland a year and a half ago to teach third grade there after my friend disappeared. I'm not from around here, but I guess I already told you that," she finished with a rueful grin.

"Does this person from Yachats, then Portland have a name to go with where she comes from?" he asked in a softer, deeper voice.

"Yes, actually, she does. My name is Jennifer Ackerly," she murmured. "But, everyone calls me Jenny."

Jenny softly groaned. She finally meets a guy who looks like a freaking god, and she can't think straight. It wasn't like her to be so flustered! Bowing her head, she let her hair hide her face—which was pretty much the same color as her hair at the moment—and wished for the ground to open up and swallow her.

A soft gasp escaped her when she felt the slide of rough fingertips along her jaw, slowly lifting her chin upward until she was forced to open her eyes. Gazing into the intense green eyes, she felt her insides melt again. A slow, goofy smile curved her lips when she saw him staring down at her with an intensity that took her breath away.

This..., she thought, *is someone I could wake up next to for the rest of my life.*

∼

Orion gazed down at the delicate face he held tenderly in the palm of his hand. He had listened intently to her as she explained who she was and where she came from, and he did not recognize either Yachats, Oregon, or this Portland. One thing he did know, they were not part of the Seven Kingdoms. He had met each of the other species from the different Isles. Jenny Ackerly was different from them. Orion couldn't ever remember having such an instant physical reaction to another person the way he had reacted to Jenny. It confused and intrigued him at the same time.

This..., he thought as he lowered his head, *is someone I could wake up next to for the rest of my life.*

Orion brushed a kiss against her soft, parted lips and quickly became lost. A wave of fiery passion exploded inside him when she opened and returned his kiss with the same fire that colored her hair. A soft moan escaped both of them, mingling their breaths together.

Astonishment washed through Orion when he felt the slender threads binding his heart inside a cocoon slowly unravel. He swore he could feel the threads release and stretch outward as if yearning to wrap Jenny in their bonds. A wave of energy coursed through his veins, making him feel invincible.

Sliding the fingers of his right hand into her hair, he wound his left arm around her waist to pull her tightly against him. Pleasure flooded through him when she wrapped her arms around his neck and continued to kiss him just as desperately as he was kissing her. They were both panting by the time she reluctantly ended the kiss. She leaned back far enough to gaze up at him with wide, shocked eyes.

"Wow!" she whispered. "That was just– Wow!"

Orion's lips pulled up at the corners. "I do not know this word you use, but I think it means you felt the same thing that I did," he admitted with a bemused smile.

Jenny tilted her head to the side and grinned. "Did you feel the ground tremble and shake?" she asked with a teasing grin.

An unexpected chuckle escaped Orion. Yes, he had felt the ground tremble and shake when she kissed him and more. Running his fingers through her hair, he stared in amazement at the curtain of red fire.

"I am Orion, by the way. I guess I should have introduced myself to you first before kissing you," he murmured in a soft voice. "I rule this kingdom."

"I kind-of figured who you were when the boys called you father," she replied with a sigh. "The boys also told me that they wanted a mother and that you needed a bride. I honestly don't know what is going on. If you haven't figured it out yet, I'm not from around here. I don't even know where here is," she whispered, looking over his shoulder toward the glittering garden and the dome covering the city. "I was just walking along the beach when I saw Dolph run into the water. I was afraid he would drown and went after him. The next thing I knew, I was here."

Orion's mouth tightened when she pulled free and wrapped her arms around her waist. She turned away from him to walk over to the windows. A worried frown pulled at his brow when he heard her release a long, deep sigh.

There was only one other person he knew who was aware of the portals between their world and another—his cousin. After their experience as teens, his father had cast a spell upon the pool, closing it to all but the small sea dragons. Magna would have had to use the Eye of the Sea Serpent, along with a very powerful spell, to open it.

Without the stone Kapian had retrieved, his cousin's magic would once again be limited to only what she was capable of creating. Dread filled him and his lips tightened when he thought of the price such a spell would cost his eldest son. Fear for his Dolph swept through him.

Walking over to her, he placed his hands on her arms. He wanted to pull her back into his arms in an effort to comfort her. She briefly stiffened before she relaxed against him.

"Jenny...," Orion started to say when the sound of a knock on the door drew his attention.

Orion glanced over his shoulder in frustration at the door. Out of the corner of his eye, he saw Jenny turn to look at the door as well. Her face was pale but composed. Her chin lifted, and she straightened her shoulders. Once again, a shaft of unfamiliar emotion swept through him.

When did life become so complicated, he wondered in resignation when the knock came again, this time louder than before.

CHAPTER SEVEN

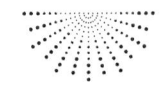

"*E*nter!" Orion ordered.

He stepped back and turned, shifting slightly so that his body was between the door and Jenny. Kapian shot him a questioning glance when he entered the room. It was obvious from his friend's curious expression that the news of his sons' unusual guest had already spread through the palace.

"So, it is true," Kapian said, glancing over Orion's shoulder.

Irritation swept through Orion when he saw the glimmer of appreciation and curiosity cross Kapian's face. Once again, he was surprised by the intense emotion that he felt in regard to Jenny. He quickly determined the flash of irritation was another new emotion for him —jealousy.

"What is it?" Orion demanded in a cutting tone. "I said we would meet later."

Orion watched as Kapian's eyes widened in surprise at his tone. He shook his head at Kapian even as his hand unconsciously moved to pull Jenny further behind him. He didn't miss the change of expression on Kapian's face or the slightly worried frown that creased his friend's brow.

"You have a visitor," Kapian replied, glancing again at Jenny. "Magna is here and she is demanding to speak with you."

Orion's face darkened. He had anticipated Magna's visit, but not quite so soon. Juno's fifth year celebration was not for another two days. He expected his cousin to appear to make her demands, but not until the last moment when he would have no other choice but to agree to accept her as his bride or choose another before midnight two days hence.

"I will see her in the throne room," Orion ordered with a dark look.

Kapian glanced at Jenny before turning his own dark gaze back to Orion. "Magna has demanded that you bring Dolph with you. She says he owes her payment, and she has come to collect," he added.

The dread Orion had felt earlier returned. When Kelia had told him what Dolph had done, he'd feared his son had made a costly bargain that would change his life forever. Orion's only hope was that Magna had not required Dolph to sign a blood oath. If his son had, and Orion could not find a way to break the spell binding Dolph to Magna, he would have no choice but to offer his life in exchange.

His mind whirled even as he nodded to Kapian. He started to take a step toward the door when he felt a slender hand on his arm. Turning, he looked back at Jenny.

"This has to do with Dolph being on the beach and with me being here, doesn't it?" she asked in a quiet voice, noticing the look of worry in Orion's eyes.

"Yes," Orion responded with a short nod. "And more. The Sea Witch is a powerful opponent and only she would have been willing to grant Dolph his wish."

"Surely she understands that making a deal with a child is unacceptable," Jenny reasoned.

Orion wished it was that simple, but it wasn't. His cousin lived in the deepest, darkest recesses of the ocean, long ago banished by his father to spend her days in the dark void for her part in inciting the war between the different kingdoms. While he wished his father could have done more, his cousin had invoked an ancient law preventing his father, a blood heir to the throne, from killing another blood heir.

"I must find out what Dolph has done," Orion explained. "If he gave a blood oath, then I have no choice but to listen to her demands."

"May I come?" Jenny asked. "If it has anything to do with me, I think I should be there. I also think it would help Dolph to know that we will both be there for him."

Orion paused for a moment, his mind racing through possible scenarios. For a brief moment, indecision pulled at him. Jenny did not understand the laws of the Seven Kingdoms. A brief flash of Dolph and Juno's anxious faces swept through his mind. Jenny was right—this did also concern her. Drawing in a deep breath, Orion turned to face her again.

"Jenny," he said, pausing as he thought what he should tell her. Raising his hand, he gently touched her cheek and looked at her with an expression of regret. "If what I suspect has happened, I need you to say yes when I ask you a question. It is imperative not only to Dolph's future but to the future of my people and kingdom as well. What I will ask of you will change your life from this day forth."

He watched as a crooked, uneasy smile lifted the corner of Jenny's mouth. He liked that she didn't automatically agree but thought carefully about his words. He had much to learn about her, just as she did about him and his people, but something told him that she would not shy away from such a challenge.

"I think that happened about three hours ago," she replied. "What is it that I have to say 'yes' to?"

Lowering his head, Orion pulled her close to his side and bent to murmur in her ear. He felt her stiffen in surprise and shock at his softly spoken words, but she didn't protest. Glancing back up, he nodded to Kapian.

"Dolph and Juno are with Kelia. Find them and meet me in the throne room," he ordered.

Orion could feel Jenny tremble when he grasped her hand and guided her out of his living quarters. It was a crazy plan, one that he wasn't sure would work. It was possible that Magna had discovered that they had located and retrieved the eye she had stolen and she would demand that he turn over the trident to her. He would have felt more confident of that if she had not also demanded that Dolph be present.

He slowed his pace when he heard Jenny draw in a deep breath. The grip she had on his hand was surprisingly strong. He winced and caressed his thumb across the back of her hand in reassurance. She shot him an apologetic smile and loosened her grip.

"Sorry, sudden nervous habit, I guess," she murmured as they walked down one long corridor after another.

"I...," Orion started to say before he stopped when he saw Kapian with Kelia and the boys by the entrance to the throne room. He paused a few feet away and turned to look down at her. Lifting a hand, he gently brushed it across her pale cheek. "There is a small room to the side when we enter. Wait there. If, and only if, I need you, I will call. I promise to do everything I can not to involve you in my family and my kingdom's troubles, Jenny."

Jenny smiled up at him with a crooked grin. "No worries. Saving kingdoms are all in a day's work. Just call Jenny's Kingdom Savers. We run specials every Monday," she joked before shaking her head in disgust. "I've totally lost my mind. I think I was around Carly for too long. Please, ignore me."

Orion chuckled and leaned down to brush a tender kiss across her pursed lips. "Now where would the fun be in that?" he replied.

He pulled back and stepped away from Jenny. Despite the tenseness of the moment, he felt confident. He would deal with his cousin once and for all. Magna had broken the ancient law that prevented him from punishing her when she had returned to the palace a few weeks ago. Today, he would force his cousin to undo the dark magic that she'd used to imprison the dragons before he ended her miserable life.

"Dolph, come with me. Juno, stay with Jenny and Kelia. Kapian... if Magna tries to escape, get Dolph to safety. I will take care of my cousin," Orion ordered.

"Yes, Your Majesty," Kapian replied.

Orion nodded to Kapian when he bowed his head and stepped away. He knew Kapian would enter through the main doors of the throne room while he and the others entered through an entrance reserved for the royal family. Stepping closer to his eldest son, he knelt down and placed his hands on Dolph's thin shoulders.

Jenny carefully watched Orion's expressions as he quietly spoke to Dolph. She only caught a few of the words, but it was enough to make her stomach tighten. Oath, spell, blood, contract... It didn't take a scientist to figure out what was going on. She had read enough fairy tales to her students to understand what those words could mean. The fact that this was really happening only made the situation seem even more bizarre—and dangerous. The tight look of concern on Orion's face and the fear in Dolph's eyes made her want to reach out to both of them and wrap her arms around them.

His expression grim but determined, Orion stood up and placed his hand on Dolph's shoulder. He glanced at her over his shoulder, and she nodded in encouragement. It was hard seeing the flicker of uncertainty in his gaze before he masked it. She couldn't help but feel he was just as confused by the feelings passing between them as she was. Throw in everything else that was happening and she would have sworn she'd awakened in a Tim Burton movie.

Jenny quietly followed Orion and Dolph through the ornately carved wooden door. She stood in the shadows of a small alcove not far from the entrance. She would be able to see and hear everything going on from this vantage point without being seen herself.

A wry smile curved her lips when she saw Orion nod to Dolph before he sat down on the large throne in the center of the platform. The guy was not only sexy as all get-out, but smart too. This Magna lady would be on a lower level than him and at a disadvantage.

The look of determination in both their eyes helped push away the doubt she had and gave her more confidence in her decision to accept what she might have to do. She swallowed and raised a trembling hand to her brow to push away a strand of hair. When Orion said her life would be different from this day forward, he hadn't been joking.

Her eyes wandered over Orion again. A shiver ran through her body, and she could feel heat course through her as she studied him. There was definitely an intense physical reaction to the man that she had never felt before toward another guy, including her ex-lovers.

The sound of the doors opening and the sight of Orion's jaw tightening warned her that his unwelcome visitor had arrived. Jenny's eyes widened when she saw a slight color change in Orion's skin. Muted shades of green, yellow, and silver ran up the side of his neck and along his right cheek. The change in color highlighted the thin, three inch line, almost like a scar, running along the column.

Gills? she wondered in awe.

Orion's broad shoulders stiffened, and his face hardened into a mask of cold indifference that sent a shiver through her. In the background, she heard the faint sound of footsteps against the smooth limestone tiles that made up the floor of the throne room. Jenny bit her lip when she heard Dolph emit a soft whimper of pain.

"Stop!" Orion growled in an icy tone, slowly rising from his seat.

A malevolent cackle echoed loudly in the room. Jenny's fingers curled into a tight fist. She couldn't see the woman's face, but the sound of her enjoyment of Dolph's pain was enough to make her want to do a fist-plant against the woman's mouth.

"He is mine, Orion," the woman replied in a quiet voice.

"No, he isn't!" Orion snarled. "Even you should have more honor than to trick a child."

Jenny took a quiet step to the side, just far enough to see the bottom of the throne platform between the pillars concealing her. For a moment, her stomach twisted in pain at the sight of the beautiful woman standing in front of Orion. The woman's rich black hair hung like a curtain down to her waist. Her gaunt face was pale, almost the color of a shimmering white pearl. Her lips were painted as black as her hair, making them stand out. She was taller than Jenny by at least a foot and was slender to the point of being emaciated. A stark white gown encased her lithe form, making Jenny's blouse and trouser clad figure look painfully underdressed.

"You should have taught him to be more careful, Orion," Magna replied. "He is reckless, like his father. That will change when I become his mother."

"*Never!*" Orion snapped, taking a step forward. "Release him, Magna. I warn you, I won't let you take my son."

Magna smirked up at Orion. "You can't stop me," she replied in a soft, confident voice. "I have his signature in blood. I control his destiny, and now yours. Accept me back into the kingdom as your bride, Orion, or I will take him as my own. Time is running out. If you have not claimed a bride in less than two days' time, I will challenge you for the kingdom. Accept me and you can keep both your son and the kingdom, deny me and you will lose everything, Orion."

"I have chosen a bride," Orion stated in a cold voice. "Your claim on my son and the kingdom is negated."

Magna's eyes flashed with rage before they cleared. The smile that Jenny was beginning to hate pulled at the woman's lips again. The witch with a capital 'B' might be beautiful on the outside, but she was about as nasty as it came on the inside.

"That is not the way it works, Orion," Magna informed him, slowly climbing the steps. "If you take a bride other than me, you will retain your place as king, but lose your son," she said with mock sympathy. Magna waved her left hand and the contract with Dolph's scribbled first name signed in blood on it appeared. "Read the fine print."

Orion held out his right hand and waited as the contract floated through the air to him. Jenny drew in a swift breath at the obvious magic and watched as he carefully unrolled the scroll and read it. His face darkened at first before his expression cleared. His upper lip curled into a sneer of triumph and he carefully rolled the scroll. Hope filled Jenny when he looked back at Magna.

"The contract states that Dolph must return with a bride for me, a mother for him and Juno, and he has. Both Dolph and the kingdom will remain mine, Magna," Orion stated.

Magna shook her head. "Read the very, very fine print," she chirped with a glimmer of malicious glee in her eyes. "To be specific, Dolph was to return with a female from another world with hair the color of fire. The female must come of her own free will and agree to be your bride before midnight of Juno's fifth year of life. You are good, Orion, but not even you can save your son. The only way to do so is to accept me as your bride."

"I did read the very, very fine print, Magna. Jenny," Orion called out, never taking his eyes off of Magna. "Come stand at my side."

Jenny trembled and swallowed. Now was not the time to chicken out, she quietly told herself. Straightening her shoulders, she smoothed her hand over her hair. Drawing in a deep, steadying breath, she stepped out from behind the pillar and pasted a smile on her lips. A surge of glee swept through Jenny when she saw Magna turn and stare at her in stunned disbelief.

Take that, bitch! she couldn't help silently crowing.

Tossing her head, she grinned at Dolph when his eyes lit up. A sense of calm settled over her as she walked closer to where he was standing next to Orion. Her chin lifted when Orion reached out his hand to her. Jenny threaded her fingers through his and squeezed his hand to let him know that he needn't worry about what she would do. Turning to face Magna, she locked gazes with the other woman.

"Hi, I'm the fire-haired woman from another world that came of her own free will to be Orion's bride before Juno's fifth birthday," Jenny announced with a grin. "I think that just about covers all of the 'very, very fine print', doesn't it, Orion?"

A smothered chuckle escaped Kapian who had come up to stand near the bottom of the steps behind Magna. Jenny knew her eyes were twinkling with amusement when she glanced up at Orion.

"Yes, I think it does," he replied with a soft chuckle.

Jenny nodded when he squeezed her hand once more before he released it to turn his full attention back to Magna. She didn't miss the hard expression he directed at the woman standing with her fists clenched or the sharp glance he shot at the man standing behind her. Jenny blanched at the unnatural swirls of dark color that had changed the woman's eyes.

"This isn't over," Magna snarled, glaring at Jenny before turning her gaze back to Orion. "As long as the Eyes of the Sea Serpent are missing, I will fight for control of the Isle of the Sea Serpent."

Orion reached into the pocket of his black trousers and pulled out a brown bag. Jenny drew in a swift breath when he took a menacing step forward. He opened the bag and tilted it. A small, familiar stone fell out of it. Her eyes widened when he held up the stone. Her gaze darted back and forth between Orion, the stone in his hand, and Magna's face. If the woman had been furious before, it was nothing compared to what she was now.

"How? It is impossible!" Magna roared, trying to reach out and snatch the smooth stone out of Orion's hand. "You dared to enter the abyss? You have no idea what you have done!"

"No, you have no idea of what you have done, Magna," Orion stated in a cold, hard voice. "You were banished to the depths, cousin, you should have stayed there. You leave me no choice but to prevent you from doing more harm to the world. If you reverse the spell you cast upon the dragons, I will spare your life and banish you to live out the last of your days imprisoned in the tower above the water."

"You do not need to imprison her, Your Majesty," Kapian said with a wry grin, fingering the sword at his side. "I would be happy to take care of her once and for all."

"You may have one of the stones, but the other is still missing," Magna whispered, staring at the stone in his hand. She glanced back and forth between Orion and Kapian. "I will locate it, and when I do, I will make sure that they are never together. He will rule the entire Isle of the Sea Serpent one day, as well as the other kingdoms. He will not stop until he has devoured all of you," she declared before closing her eyes and softly muttering a string of words too faint for Jenny to hear.

"Orion!" Kapian shouted, rushing up the steps.

"Magna, stop!" Orion demand, thrusting his hand out and calling out a command.

Long tentacles shot out from around Magna and an inhuman cry of rage echoed through the room. Jenny reached one hand up to cover her ear while she wrapped her arm around Dolph's waist and pulled him backwards when one of the black bands reached toward him. Jenny twisted and pulled Dolph down, covering him protectively with her body.

A loud scream pierced the air. Jenny's head snapped up, and she looked frantically in front of her. Her arms tightened around Dolph when she saw the long tentacle that had struck out at them lying on the floor, writhing before it dissolved. Her lips parted when she saw the dark scorched mark left behind. Turning her head, she saw Orion and Kapian fighting the lightning-fast bands swirling around Magna. The woman no longer looked beautiful. For a brief moment, Magna's gaze and hers locked. She saw an expression that looked confusingly like despair in the woman's eyes before they hardened again.

"You cannot kill him, Orion," Magna cried out.

Jenny drew in a hissing breath when the blades of Orion and Kapian's swords passed through the stream of black bubbles where Magna had been standing. The other woman was gone. Jenny glanced down when she felt a small hand slide into hers and Dolph wiggled under her. Glancing up once more to make sure it was safe, she rolled to the side and sat up. Dolph sat up beside her and glanced around with bright, wary eyes before he turned back to look at her.

"Is she gone?" he asked.

Jenny's gaze followed Orion and Kapian as they turned in a tight circle on the steps where Magna had been. The only evidence that Magna had been there was the scorch mark on the pristine limestone, but even that was beginning to fade. A movement out of the corner of her eye showed that Kelia, Coralus, and Juno had stepped out of the alcove.

"Yes, I think so," Jenny finally replied.

"You will stay?" Dolph anxiously asked, staring up at her. "You'll be our mother?"

"Oh, Dolph...," Jenny murmured.

She opened her arms. Dolph quickly crawled into them. Resting her chin on his head, she glanced around the large room. How could she give him an answer? In the course of an afternoon her life had gone from grief to resolve in moving on to something out of a fairy tale. Once again, she couldn't help but wonder if this could have been what happened to Carly.

"Jenny."

Orion's voice broke through her reverie, and she glanced up at him. He silently held out his hand. She released her hold on Dolph and reached up. Dolph slid off her lap and stood. A moment later, Jenny was standing in front of Orion. She swallowed at the intense, troubled expression on his face.

"What...?" Jenny started to ask.

Her voice died when Dolph stepped close to her left side while Juno came to stand next to her right. She could feel the younger boy's hand grip the end of her shirt. Her lips parted to protest, but she knew that there was nothing she could say that would change the course she was on. Her fate had been decided the moment she followed Dolph into the water.

"I need you to say yes. Yes, for my kingdom. Yes, for my people. Yes... that you will agree to be my bride," Orion said in a quiet voice.

"Father, you forgot to say yes to being our mother," Juno interjected, twisting his small hand in Jenny's shirt.

Orion's lips twitched, and he gave Jenny a rueful smile. "And yes to being the mother of my two wayward sons who like to get into far too much mischief for their own good," he solemnly added.

A soft chuckle escaped Jenny and her eyes twinkled with their own mischief. "Wayward, huh? Sounds like they need someone who can keep up with them," she teased.

"Oh, they are very wayward," Kelia said. "They will need someone very special, my lady."

"Someone who likes to play games, right, Dolph? Lots of fun games with us," Juno asked, looking around at his brother.

"And who can love us," Dolph added.

Tears filled Jenny's eyes at the flash of uncertainty in Dolph's eyes. She would need some time to get used to things. Being a teacher in a classroom full of kids was a whole lot different than being a mom.

Well, maybe not a whole lot, she thought ruefully. *Being a teacher was more like skipping parenthood and going straight to being a grandparent—and at the end of the day I was able to give them back to their parents.*

"Yes," Jenny replied, looking up at Orion. "Yes, to all of the above."

Juno's squeal of happiness rang through the air, and he wrapped his arms around her waist. She glanced down into the little boy's bright green eyes that were glowing with happiness. She silently groaned and closed her eyes. Sucker! She had to have the biggest 'Sucker' neon sign attached to her forehead in the entire universe. Carly used to laugh and say there was only one person in the world who was a bigger pushover than she was and that was Jenny. It was now official.

CHAPTER EIGHT

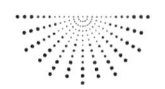

"You know, when I said you needed to find a bride, I honestly never expected you to find one like this," Kapian stated, leaning back against the wall.

"It isn't like I have a choice in the matter. You heard Magna," Orion bit out, growling when he realized he had buttoned his vest wrong.

"Yes, the fine print," Kapian replied with a nod and a grin.

Orion shot a glare at his friend. "The very, very fine print. Have you ever seen a woman with hair the color of fire coral before?" he asked.

"Naturally? No. I have seen a few on the Isle of the Pirates, but it was more orange. I wonder where she came from?" Kapian asked, rubbing his chin with a thoughtful expression.

"When were you on the Isle of the Pirates?" Orion asked in surprise.

Kapian shook his head. "A few weeks ago. I heard that Ashure was racing sea stags again," he dryly replied.

Orion grimaced. "I swear the man does nothing but try to irritate the rest of us. He knows that it is forbidden to capture the stags," he replied.

Kapian shrugged. "You know Ashure. The man will do anything for excitement and a few credits," he answered.

"He will start another war if he is not careful," Orion retorted.

"He'd probably have bets placed on that as well," Kapian joked.

Orion pursed his lips and nodded. Ashure would not only place bets, but the damn pirate king would probably have rigged the battles in his favor. If there wasn't so much going on at the moment, he would challenge Ashure to a race—with the kingdom of the Isle of the Pirates as the prize. After a moment's thought of what that would entail, a shudder ran through Orion.

Ashure having to rule over that lot of misfits is enough punishment for anyone. Perhaps I should send Magna to him instead of killing her, Orion silently thought.

"Perhaps your father should have banished Magna there. I'm sure Ashure would have loved dealing with her. Speaking of Magna, what are we going to do about your cousin?" Kapian asked in a grim tone.

Orion glanced at his friend. "We have been around each other too long. I was thinking the same thing. Let me get through this evening. I want to make sure the blood oath that Dolph signed is terminated, then I will focus on stopping Magna once and for all," he replied with a sigh before pulling on the long coat draped across the chair near him and turned to face Kapian with a wary expression. "Now, how do I look?"

Kapian cast an assessing gaze at him. Orion could feel the scowl darkening his features when his friend remained silent. Reaching up, he adjusted the collar of the coat he had slipped on.

"Like a king about to be married," Kapian finally replied.

Orion nodded and glanced outside. Darkness had fallen above the seas. Shafts of moonlight struck the upper dome and tiny dots of luminous green lights twinkled and swirled in the current that flowed over the clear ceiling. Stars under the sea—a sight that Orion had always loved.

"What if she changes her mind? She knows nothing about our world—or of me," Orion murmured, turning to quietly look out the window.

"You know nothing of her, either. The Goddess works in mysterious ways. Dolph said the water told him where to find Jenny. I have to believe the Goddess was giving you a sign," Kapian pointed out.

Orion turned when he heard the knock on the door to his bedroom. Kapian opened the door and quietly spoke to Coralus. The older man caught Orion's gaze, smiled, and bowed his head before stepping back.

"Well, it appears your bride hasn't disappeared, so you have one less thing to worry about," Kapian informed him with a grin.

Orion swallowed and nodded. Wrapping his hand around the end of his sword, he started forward when Kapian opened the door all the way and stood to the side to let him pass. He paused in the doorway, straightened his shoulders, and drew in a deep breath. At least he had known Shamill before he married her, not that it had made much of a difference when it came to the lack of fire between them in their union.

The memory of the fire of desire that swept through him when he saw Jenny, then the intensity of their kiss made his body harden. It was going to be a very, very long and difficult few weeks—he refused to think in the terms of months—if just the thought of her brought his body to such an awakening he would need every bit of his self-control not to make a fool of himself.

For the first time in years, excitement built up inside him. He would court Jenny, get to know her, and build a fire between them that not even the waters of the ocean would be able to put out. Already a plan was forming in his mind. There were many wonders under the sea to be seen and explored. With Dolph and Juno's help, they would capture Jenny's heart and ensure that she would never want to return to her world.

"What's wrong?" Kapian asked.

Orion's lips twitched and he shook his head. "Nothing," he said before walking out of the room.

"He is a good man, Lady Jenny," Kelia informed Jenny for the hundredth time as she braided her hair.

"You've already said that," Jenny replied, lifting a shaking hand to her flushed cheek.

"He loves his sons and his people," Kelia added.

Jenny watched as Kelia began tucking dozens of tiny vibrant gold flowers in the braid. Kelia had been trying to reassure Jenny that Orion was a wonderful man ever since she guided her back to the guest bedroom in his living quarters. She dropped her hand to her lap and nervously fingered the silky, light-green dress that she was wearing.

The dress was magnificent. Small, jade-colored shell buttons embellished the top of the gown down to the waist, and flowers fashioned from thousands of tiny amber beads that blossomed on golden stems with matching leaves adorned the hem. She felt like she was playing dress up for one of the yearly Renaissance festivals that she used to attend with Carly.

"Kelia, have you ever heard of any other unusual women appearing in your world? Someone like me?" Jenny asked, gazing at Kelia in the mirror.

Kelia's hands stilled for a moment, and she looked thoughtful. After a few seconds, the older woman shook her head. Disappointment pierced through Jenny.

"No, why do you ask?" Kelia replied.

To hide the tears of disappointment, Jenny averted her eyes by looking down at the items on the table in front of her. Damn, but she was an emotional wreck at the moment. Of course, she couldn't help thinking that discovering you're in an alternate reality and getting married to a king all on the same day could have something to do with it.

"No reason, I was just curious," Jenny said, unable to mention Carly's name without fear of bursting into tears.

"After the disappearance of the King and Queen, then the death of Lady Shamill, I feared Lord Orion would never find happiness. I have known him all of his life, and he has always been such a wonderful man. I was his nursemaid from the time he was born until Coralus took him under his wing after the old King's request to start training him. The two princes remind me so much of Orion when he was younger. His Majesty, Sir Kapian, and that cousin of his were always getting into mischief. It is such a shame Magna turned out the way she did. She had always been such a sweet girl when she was younger. If I may be so forward as to say, Coralus and I think of His Majesty with as much affection as we do our own children. All done now. If I may say so, Lady Jenny, you are beautiful," Kelia said with a satisfied sigh.

Jenny gave Kelia a weak smile before staring at her reflection in the mirror. If she didn't know any better, she'd swear she was looking at a stranger instead of her own image. On impulse, Jenny reached up and touched the smooth, cool glass just to make sure.

It really is me, she thought in amazement.

Her reflection in the mirror drew in a swift breath. For the past hour, one part of Jenny's brain had been silently listening to Kelia, picking out interesting pieces of information, sorting them, and then storing them for future use. At the same time, the other part of her brain was in the middle of having a major meltdown. Now, the fog had evaporated, and everything became crystal clear—she was about to marry a man she met just a few hours ago—a man from another world—a man who lived under the sea.

"What am I doing?" Jenny whispered, pulling her hand back from the glass.

In the reflection, she saw Kelia's expression soften in understanding. Jenny felt the chair she was in turn until she was facing the older woman. Kelia knelt down in front of Jenny and gently cupped her hands.

"You are saving a kingdom from certain destruction. You are saving the life of a young boy who would do anything to find a mother for himself and his brother and a woman who could make his father happy. You are giving a wonderful man a chance to save his people and his family," Kelia said.

Confusion darkened Jenny's eyes. "But... What about my life? My home? I...." Jenny's voice faded.

"You would not be here if the Goddess hadn't known that you were meant to be here," Kelia responded in a confident voice.

"How can you be so sure?" Jenny asked.

"Did you leave someone you love behind in your world?" Kelia asked.

"No," Jenny replied.

"Is there anything in your world that you will miss more than life itself?" Kelia asked.

Jenny could feel her head shaking no even before Kelia had finished asking her question. The only things Jenny had left behind were materialistic items. There was no family who would miss her. She had a handful of friends who would wonder what had happened to her, but not enough to come looking for answers like she had for Carly. She had no boyfriends or ex-lovers who ever cared enough to keep in touch.

"No," she whispered, bowing her head.

"You already have the hearts of two young boys. Personally, I don't think it will be that difficult to capture the heart of their father either if you give him a chance. That is all they ask for, Lady Jenny, a chance to get to know them—a chance for you to accept this world," Kelia replied as she stood up and pulled Jenny out of her chair.

A rueful smile curved Jenny's lips. "How did you get so good at this?" she asked.

Kelia's eyes twinkled with delight. "I have children of my own and have been around His Majesty and the young princes long enough to know how to read people," she chuckled.

"I can't believe I'm going to do this," Jenny admitted, fingering the fine material of her dress again.

"I have a feeling King Orion will be wondering how he is going to keep his hands off of you through the ceremony once he sees how lovely you are," Kelia teased.

Jenny could feel the blush wash up into her cheeks. Her thoughts immediately turned to the kiss they shared that afternoon. A shaft of desire swept through her, and she could feel the warmth spread up to her core. Just the thought of the man made her want to do things she had only read about in her romance books.

"Who knows, maybe it will be you that has the difficulty," Kelia teased.

"Oh, be quiet," Jenny muttered, fanning her face with her hand.

Kelia laughed and stood back so Jenny could go ahead of her. Jenny grinned at the older woman. Clutching the material of the gown in her hands, she lifted it just far enough to make sure she didn't step on it before raising her chin and straightening her shoulders. She was going to do this.

"I've totally lost my mind," she said, staring at the door and willing her legs to work.

"Completely, so you have nothing to worry about," Kelia informed her.

Jenny started walking when she felt Kelia's hand against the small of her back, pressing her forward. The doubts coursing through her faded when the door opened, and she saw Dolph and Juno standing outside waiting for her. Dolph looked solemn while Juno had a huge grin on his face. Both boys looked dashing in their formal attire of dark brown trousers, matching vests and coats, and pristine white shirts.

"You two look awesome," Jenny said, nodding with approval.

"You look like a princess," Juno exclaimed with a grin.

"She will be a Queen soon enough. I take it you two boys are here to escort her," Kelia said in a firm voice.

"Yes," Dolph replied.

Jenny's face lit up with delight when Dolph took a step forward and bowed. He kept one hand behind his back and the other swept forward across his stomach. When he straightened, he held out his arm. Only when Jenny extended her hand did he turn to stand next to her left side. Jerking his head at his brother, he waited for a moment before speaking.

"Juno, remember what Coralus told us," Dolph muttered under his breath.

"What? Oh! Yes, I forgot," Juno replied. "Sorry, Jenny."

Jenny's lips curved into a reassuring smile when Juno stepped up in front of her and bowed. He wasn't as graceful or confident as his older brother, but he more than made up for it with his adorable grin. She couldn't help but curtsy to the little boy when he held out his arm to her. His infectious giggles soon had all of them, including Dolph, laughing.

"I would like a little sister," Juno said excitedly. "I hope she has fire hair like you do. I will be a very gallant big brother and protect her from all the monsters."

"I think it might be best to wait a little while on the sister," Jenny laughed.

"How long?" Juno asked, looking up at her with hopeful eyes. "A week?"

"Juno!" Dolph hissed, glaring at his younger brother.

"What? You said you want a baby sister, too. You said it would be better than having another brother," Juno defended.

"He's young, ignore him," Dolph said with a roll of his eyes.

Jenny couldn't help the laugh that escaped. It would appear that boys were boys no matter where you are. She listened to the boys argue about who said what and when she was supposed to present them with a new sister as they walked through the corridors that were now lined with people.

Being the center of attention made her cheeks grow warm again. Lifting her chin, she tried to act like walking down an elaborate hallway in an underwater palace dressed like she was going to Cinderella's ball with two small princes as her escort was a normal, everyday thing. The smile on her lips trembled, and tears burned her eyes when a wave of self-doubt hit her hard.

What in the hell am I doing? This is totally crazy! she thought as a wave of panic swept through her.

She was about to bolt to the safety of the guest bedroom. The plan was forming in her mind. She'd get back into her own clothes, escape through the garden to the cave, and find the blasted portal back home where she was Jenny—just plain, elementary-school-teacher Jenny. Her steps faltered to a stop when two little girls stepped out in front of her and curtsied.

"For you, my lady," one of the little girls said with a shy smile.

"Thank... Thank you," Jenny said, releasing Dolph's arm to take the flowers from the little girl.

"I think you are beautiful. Will your hair burn me if I touch it?" the other little girl asked.

"Would you like to touch it and find out?" Jenny asked with a breathless laugh.

"Oh! May I?" the little girl exclaimed.

Jenny gathered her skirt in her hands and bent down so the little girl could touch her hair. She grinned when the girls' mother stepped forward with a gasp of dismay. Jenny winked at the woman who placed a hand on her brow and gave a mortified shake of her head.

"It is soft," the little girl said in excitement. "Momma, her hair doesn't burn me."

"Can I touch it too?" the older of the two girls hesitantly asked.

"Of course," Jenny said.

"Please forgive them, my lady. We have never seen hair the color of yours before," the mother said with an apologetic smile.

"I don't mind," Jenny assured the woman.

For the first time, she noticed that everyone had white, brown, or black hair. She straightened as the woman guided the two girls to stand against the wall again. Clutching the bouquet of flowers against her chest, Jenny saw the rows of smiling faces looking at her with a combination of awe, curiosity, and hope.

"This way," Dolph said, placing her hand on his arm again.

"Thank you, Dolph," Jenny murmured, starting forward again.

They continued down to the end of the corridor where two massive doors stood. The guards standing at attention pulled the doors opened. On the other side of the room was a platform with four ornate chairs sitting on it. There were three men standing on the platform. They all turned when they heard the doors, but only one of them held Jenny's attention—the one in the middle.

CHAPTER NINE

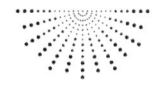

The sound of the doors opening cut short Orion's discussion with Kapian and Coralus on how to handle Ashure. Orion turned and locked eyes with Jenny. Swallowing, he didn't realize that he was holding his breath until Kapian slapped his shoulder, and he heard Coralus chuckle.

"Breathe, my friend," Kapian said. "If you don't, I'll have to stand in for you."

"Not in this lifetime," Orion automatically retorted.

"I wonder if Dolph could find out if she has a sister or a distant cousin," Kapian remarked.

Orion ignored Kapian and stepped forward. The ceremony would be short. He would ask Jenny once again if she would be his bride, his Queen, and stand by his side to help rule the Isle of the Sea Serpent. If she answered yes to each question, they would be bound together, and the balance to the kingdom would be restored.

"Relax, Your Majesty," Coralus suggested.

It took Orion a moment to realize he was standing there with his fists clenched. He drew in a deep breath and held it for several long seconds, slowly releasing it to focus on relaxing his body. His gaze swept over Jenny as she approached the throne. Workers and visitors, the people who made up his kingdom followed her in a show of support and approval of his choice.

Orion's gaze proudly took in the presence of Dolph on Jenny's left and Juno on her right. Both boys walked with their shoulders straight and their heads high. When they were within a few feet of the steps, the boys slowed so that Jenny could ascend the platform steps ahead of them.

Desire hit him hard when she reached down and lifted her skirt high enough to avoid tripping. Delicate jade slippers covered her feet. He didn't miss the glimpse of her pale ankle. His gaze swept to her face when she paused on the first step. A flush of heat made him want to pull on the collar of his shirt when he saw the amusement in her eyes. She had caught him staring.

A slow, crooked smile suddenly appeared on his face. He knew she could see the amusement and appreciation in his gaze. From the slight flush to her cheeks, she also saw the desire he didn't try to hide. A wicked grin curved her lips.

"You, my friend, are in big trouble," Kapian chuckled under his breath.

"Tell me something I don't already know," Orion retorted with a soft groan. "I hope she doesn't mind a fast courtship."

Kapian and Coralus just grinned. Orion wished he could adjust more than his collar. The heat had moved downward and was now settled firmly in his groin. He was thankful the long coat he wore hid the evidence of his discomfort.

He reached out his hand to her when she stepped up on the last step. She released her gown and took his hand. Her fingers felt chilled against his and Orion brought them to his lips to press a warm kiss against them.

"Are you sure you wish to do this?" he asked, gazing intently into her eyes.

Jenny looked up at him. His stomach clenched when she didn't immediately reply. Instead, she continued to stare up into his eyes.

"Yes," she finally replied with a radiant smile. "I'm sure."

"I want to kiss you again," Orion warned her.

"I wouldn't stop you," Jenny quipped.

A pleased smile lit her features when he groaned and tightened his fingers around her hand. He had never known a woman who didn't think twice about teasing him. He had met her only a few hours ago, but he felt like he had known her all his life. A sense of peace settled in his soul as she stepped close to him.

"Do you, Jenny Ackerly, agree to be my bride?" Orion asked in a loud voice that reverberated through the suddenly silent room.

Jenny's hand trembled in his, but she didn't look away. "Yes, I do," she said in a voice that rang loud and clear.

"Do you, Jenny Ackerly, agree to be my Queen, stand by my side as my equal, and restore balance to the Isle of the Sea Serpent and the Seven Kingdoms?" Orion asked.

"Yes, I do," Jenny replied.

"Do you, Jenny Ackerly, agree to help me guide our people, rule above and below the seas, and protect the Isle of the Sea Serpent?" he asked in a softer voice.

"Yes, I do. I will help you," Jenny said.

"I declare...," Orion started to say before he stopped at the sudden tug on his coat. "What is it Juno?" he asked with a frown.

"You forgot to ask her if she will be our mother," Juno said.

"I... That is not...," Orion started to say before he felt Jenny squeeze his hand. Glancing at her, his lips twitched when she raised an eyebrow and nodded her head. "Will you take Dolph and Juno as your sons and be a mother to them?" he asked ruefully, ignoring the sounds of smothered laughter from their observers.

"Yes, I do. I would love to take Dolph and Juno as my sons and be their mom," Jenny replied.

"I declare...," Orion started to say again when he felt another tug on his coat. Glancing back down at Juno, he released an exasperated breath. "Yes, Juno?"

"Will she play games with us?" Juno asked anxiously.

Orion glanced back at Jenny. "Will you play games with them?" he asked in a dry voice.

"Lots of games," Jenny promised.

Orion turned to look at his youngest son with a raised eyebrow. "Anything else?" he asked.

"Just one more," Juno said with a happy smile. "How long before we get a fire-haired baby sister?"

Laughter erupted throughout the room. Even Orion couldn't prevent the chuckle that escaped him. His gaze turned back to Jenny. Her cheeks were a vivid red, but her eyes twinkled with mirth.

"I'll see what I can do about that—starting very soon, hopefully," Orion murmured.

"In accordance with the laws of the Isle of the Sea Serpent, I declare our union sealed, our lives bound together, and the balance to the kingdom restored," Orion declared, turning to look out at the people watching them. He looked down at Jenny with a smile that faltered after he saw her bite her bottom lip. "What is it?"

She glanced up at him with a look of uncertainty. "Well, where I come from the ceremony usually ends with the saying 'You may now kiss the bride'," she said with a sigh.

"I don't mind if I do," Orion said with a wicked smile.

His lips covered Jenny's, capturing her gasp of surprise when he suddenly wrapped his arm around her waist and pulled her against his body. He took advantage of her parted lips to deepen the kiss. Her body stiffened for a moment before her arms swept up around his neck, and she kissed him back with an intensity that made his toes curl.

"I've never seen a ceremony end like this," Kapian muttered to Coralus.

"Maybe they are starting a new tradition," Coralus replied.

"I'm half expecting Juno's wish for a sister to be granted in front of us all," Kapian chuckled before he clamped his lips together.

Orion felt Jenny start to pull away and knew she had heard the two men. After he broke the kiss, Orion glared at the men when Jenny bowed her head and rested her forehead against his chest. He could feel her body trembling.

"Enough! I won't have you embarrassing your Queen," Orion growled.

"I sincerely apologize, Your Majesty. I meant no disrespect," Coralus said.

"I did—ouch! I mean, I didn't... mean any disrespect, that is," Kapian hastily said, after Coralus elbowed him in the ribs.

"I should have both of you...," Orion started to threaten before he felt Jenny's slender fingers against his lips.

Lifting her head, Jenny laughed. "That was good, guys. You should start your own comedy tour," she teased, before turning to look up at Orion. She tenderly rubbed the corner of Orion's mouth with her thumb. "I'd never have survived being a teacher if I couldn't take a little teasing and make a little fun of life. I'm good."

Orion nipped her thumb. "They are lucky to have you. I would have hung them in irons, otherwise," he replied.

Doubt clouded Jenny's eyes, and she turned to look at the two men. Coralus was shaking his head and Kapian was trying not to laugh. Orion grunted and groaned.

"Irons?" Jenny asked with a doubtful expression.

"Nothing to worry about, Jenny. After a few centuries the iron would corrode and they would be free again," Orion promised.

"Oh, you!"

"Behold your new Queen!" Kapian called out.

Orion turned Jenny in his arms and wrapped them around her waist. The roar of the crowd grew when Jenny motioned for the boys to come stand in front of her. Juno smiled when Jenny handed him the bouquet of flowers to hold so she could lay her hands on their shoulders.

Orion bent his head when he heard Dolph call to him. Glancing down, he saw that his oldest son had pulled back the sleeve of his coat. The mark of the blood oath he'd made with Magna faded before their eyes. The spell was broken, and Dolph was safe. Bending his head to Jenny, Orion pressed a kiss behind her left ear.

"Thank you, Jenny," he murmured in her ear.

She tilted her head back and looked up at him with a puzzled expression. He hugged her to his body, unable to express his gratitude for the selfless gift she had given him. He pressed another kiss to her lips before turning to look out at the still cheering crowd.

"What do we do now?" Jenny asked in a breathless voice.

"Celebrate!" Kapian laughed.

~

"Would you like me to take care of her?" Kelia asked.

Orion's expression softened and he shook his head. Kelia could barely stand up. In fact, he was pretty sure Coralus was supporting his exhausted wife. It was well past midnight, and the festivities inside and outside of the castle continued. News of his marriage had quickly spread throughout the kingdom. Lifting his gaze to the clear dome, he could see the fireworks exploding overhead as the isle above celebrated as well.

"No, I will see to my wife," Orion stated.

"Congratulations again, Your Majesty. Queen Jenny is a beautiful and very much needed Queen for the people of the sea," Kelia replied with a tired smile.

"Thank you, Kelia. You are truly a wonderful help to my family. Get some rest. I'm sure that Queen Jenny will need your assistance in the coming weeks as she adjusts to our world," Orion said.

"It will be a great honor to continue to be of assistance," Kelia said.

"I must get her to bed or she will be fretting over what she needs to do. Good night, Your Majesty," Coralus said.

"Good night, Coralus," Orion said.

Orion turned to look down at Jenny. A twinge of guilt pierced him when he saw her eyelashes flutter before she leaned against him and fell asleep. He had been chatting with Kapian and Coralus and lost track of time. Karin, Kelia's granddaughter, had spirited Dolph and Juno away hours ago.

With a sigh, Orion bent over and picked Jenny up in his arms. Several of the golden flowers had fallen from her braid. They lay against the red velvet of the couch they were sitting on. He nodded his thanks when Kapian silently rose from his seat and cleared a path to a recessed door.

"I'm awake," Jenny mumbled before turning her face into his chest and emitted a soft snore.

Kapian chuckled. "Even in sleep she is defiant," he teased.

"I will have to remember that," Orion said, passing through the door and into a deserted hallway.

"I will see you safely to your quarters, then bid you good night. I will also arrange for Her Majesty's private guards first thing in the morning," Kapian said.

Orion nodded. There were matters that would require his attention, but Kapian and Coralus could attend to most of them in his absence. He wanted to spend as much time with Jenny as he could.

Kapian paused several feet from the entrance to Orion's chamber. Orion's arms tightened around Jenny when he saw his friend's expression soften. Once again, the strange flash of emotion hit him.

"You are one very lucky man, my friend. I hope you know that—first Shamill, then your sons, and now Jenny. I don't know of any other man who could be so fortunate, or so worthy," Kapian said.

"You had too much wine tonight, Kapian. Go get some rest," Orion ordered.

"And you are very wise and observant, Your Majesty. I should have stopped two bottles before I did," Kapian chuckled, lifting his hand to touch his brow, he bowed his head. "Good night. May the morning come with great joy for you."

"Good night, Kapian," Orion replied with a shake of his head.

Orion didn't wait to watch his friend stagger off. He continued down the hallway. The two guards immediately opened the doors for him. Once he passed through, they were closed behind him, leaving the two of them alone for the second time since he had met her yesterday.

Crossing the living area, he headed down the hallway. He passed by several doors leading to the boys' bedrooms and the guest room until he came to his room at the end of the hallway. The door was still partially open from when he and Kapian had exited earlier. Pushing the door open, he entered and walked to the large bed centered against the far wall.

Orion carefully lowered Jenny onto the bed. He smiled when he saw the row of nearly one hundred buttons. He deeply sighed and set to work removing the bulky gown. He started with her feet, removing the jade slippers and sheer thigh-high stockings. Her legs were long and smooth.

He did his best to keep his touch impersonal, focusing on removing the clothing that would make it difficult for Jenny to get a good rest. Of course, that didn't mean his mind was staying impersonal. It had been a long time since he'd been with a woman. His focus had been on his sons and the kingdom. His reaction to Jenny confused him. He'd never felt such a primitive desire before. His relationship with Shamill had been based on mutual respect, duty, and physical release. He'd never felt any desire to stay with Shamill afterward and neither had she. With Jenny it was different, he wanted to hold her in his arms and feel the warmth of her body next to his even if that was all that was involved.

He deftly unbuttoned her gown. Underneath, she wore a thin, white silk under-slip. He swallowed when he saw her plump breasts straining against the material.

He drew in a deep breath and carefully slid an arm under her shoulders to lift her up far enough to pull the gown free. Her hips lifted off the bed when he tugged it down. She softly murmured, but he couldn't understand the words. Once free of the constricting material, she rolled over onto her side and folded her hands under her cheek.

"I must give thanks that you're either sleeping deeply or so exhausted you know not how tempting you are," Orion softly said with a shake of his head. "Goddess, but I want to feel your legs wrapped around me."

A shaft of painful desire shot through him. He pulled back the covers on the bed and lifted her up far enough to tuck her under the covers. Once she was settled, he picked up her gown and stockings and carried them over to the couch. He laid them down before removing his coat and vest and unbuttoning his shirt. Pulling off his boots, he set them to the side.

A quick glance toward the bed showed that Jenny had settled into an even deeper sleep. A wave of longing washed through him. He had a feeling it was going to take him a bit longer to fall into a restful sleep.

Turning, he walked into the attached bathroom. He took care of his personal needs before removing his shirt and trousers. With a sigh of regret, he pulled on a pair of loose fitting sleeping pants he wore in case the boys needed him at night.

He extinguished the light in the bathroom and returned to the bedroom. Jenny was lying with her back toward him, her arms around the pillow. Pulling the covers back, he slid in beside her. He reached over and wrapped his arm around her waist, pulling her close against his body.

"Carly, I had such an amazing dream," Jenny murmured in her sleep.

Orion froze. He debated on whether he should see if she would say anything else. When she didn't, he couldn't help but see if she would speak again.

"What was it about?" he softly asked.

A deep sigh escaped Jenny before she mumbled again. "Mermaids… I always wanted to be a mermaid," she replied.

Jenny released another deep sigh before her breathing slowed. He knew he wouldn't get anything else from her. His arm tightened around her and he pressed a kiss against her exposed shoulder.

Mermaids, he thought. Dolph had explained what a mermaid was to him. *I have found my own mermaid.*

Tomorrow he would begin learning about his new bride. Tonight—or what was left of it—he would just hold her. He finally relaxed as his tired mind slowed. The feel of Jenny's warm body against his, the relief from the stress of the day, and the rhythmic sound of the water from the garden falls pulled him into a deep, exhausted sleep.

On the edge of his dream, a dark shadow danced through his mind. He could see his cousin reaching out to him—her pale, trembling hands begging him for help. Her gaunt features were twisted in anguish.

Orion…. You have angered him. He seeks to destroy the other kingdoms. There is only one way to stop him. You must destroy us. Destroy me—He…. Orion!

A shudder ran through Orion's body as the nightmare of Magna calling to him dissolved. His last vision was of black tentacles reaching out to wrap around Magna's struggling figure. His breathing quickened and he started to wake until he felt the clasp of a warm hand and slender fingers. Magna's image faded and was replaced by a woman with a mischievous smile, dancing eyes the color of sea glass, and hair the color of fire coral. This time, he slipped into a deep sleep with a more pleasant dream.

CHAPTER TEN

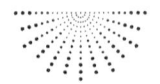

The shimmering shaft of light streaming through the windows and the sound of laughter woke Orion the next morning. He immediately reached for Jenny. He snapped up into a sitting position when he realized she was gone. He fell back against the pillows when he heard Juno's voice calling out in excitement.

"Run, Jenny!" Juno shouted.

"Safe!" Jenny called out, followed by a whoop of delight.

Orion's lips curved into a smile. He could picture her dancing. Stretching, he rubbed his hands down his face. It had been years since he had slept so hard or so late. Shaking his head in disgust, he thrust the covers back, slid from the bed, and padded to the bathroom.

Twenty minutes later, he pulled on his shirt, buttoning it as he walked to the balcony doors across from the bed. Stepping outside, he walked to the railing and looked out over the garden. He gripped the pillar and watched the small group below.

Jenny had her hair gathered up with a long section hanging down. She was wearing a strange shirt and a pair of blue trousers that must have been from her world. Karin was standing by a large white square with her skirt hiked up in both hands. Coralus had a ball. Jenny was on another white square—or rather, dancing on and off it while Coralus kept glancing over his shoulder at her with a playful scowl.

"Roll the ball, Father. I cannot kick it if you won't roll it," Karin shouted in exasperation.

"If I do, she will run and you will get another point. We are already behind by three," Coralus retorted.

"That's because Jenny is a pro kickball player, right Jenny?" Dolph said with a grin.

"I am the greatest kickball player in all of the Seven Kingdoms," Jenny replied.

"That is because you are the only one who understands how to play this game," Kapian retorted. "Roll the ball, Coralus."

Coralus grumbled and rolled the ball. Jenny took off before it even left his hands. Orion watched as Jenny raced for another white square. Karin kicked the ball low to the ground. Coralus dove for it and missed. Kapian ran forward and scooped it up. By now, Jenny had touched the other base while Karin ran for the first white square.

Orion gripped the railing when he saw Kapian bend his arm back. It was quickly evident that his friend was going to throw the ball at Jenny. The shout of denial died on his lips, and anger burst through him when the ball soared through the air toward Jenny. He watched in astonishment as she twisted at the last second, and the ball flew by her.

Dolph and Juno were already racing for the ball while Coralus and Kapian groaned, and the women cheered. Jenny raised her arms in the air as she touched the white square where Karin was standing only a moment before. Karin raced around the squares while Dolph and Juno fought over who would throw the ball.

"Yes! Home run!! Girls rule, guys drool! We are the champions!" Jenny shouted in glee, dancing around. "Whoop, whoop, whoop! We are the champions—of the underwater world!"

Laughter rang through the garden as Jenny danced around in a circle while waving her arms and kicking her long legs up. Karin threw her arms around Jenny, her flushed face glowing from her run. Kelia was clapping while Kapian bent to help Coralus up off the ground, and Dolph and Juno continued arguing over who should have thrown the ball.

"You should have thrown the ball at Karin," Dolph said, looking at Kapian. "She would have been easier to get out, and we only needed one more."

"I think there is a problem with the ball," Kapian complained.

"The only problem is with your aim. I thought I taught you better. Maybe you need some remediation," Coralus chuckled, slapping Kapian on the shoulder.

"Father! Jenny taught us a new game. Did you see how fast she can run?" Juno exclaimed when he saw Orion watching them.

"Yes. I also saw Kapian try to hit her with the ball," Orion stated, looking pointedly at his Captain of the Guard.

Kapian pointed at Jenny. "She said it was part of the game. Besides, I didn't throw it that hard," he said defensively.

Orion shook his head at his friend. Turning, he followed the balcony to a set of stairs leading down into the garden. He paused at the bottom when he saw Jenny walking toward him. She smiled shyly up at him. Her face was flushed from her excitement but grew even rosier as she stared up at him.

"I missed you when I woke," he said without thinking.

"I... Yes, that was a bit of a surprise," she said with a small laugh.

He followed her hand with his gaze as she raised it to brush a loose strand of red hair from her face. He reached up and caught it. The fire that had started yesterday ignited when he noticed her pupils dilate when he lifted her fingers to his lips.

"I'm hungry," Juno announced behind them.

"I'll take the boys in for some refreshments," Kelia said.

"Thank you, Kelia. We will follow shortly," Orion said, not pulling his gaze away from Jenny's.

"We'll help you," Coralus stated.

Orion waited until the small group disappeared down one of the paths leading to the main section of the palace. Once they were alone, he slid his other hand around Jenny's waist and pulled her close. Her breathing increased, but she didn't pull away from him. His body reacted to her response, his cock growing hard.

"I wanted to kill Kapian when I saw him throw that ball at you," he admitted in a rough voice.

"It was just a game. It is how you play it," she said.

"I didn't like waking with you gone," he stated.

Jenny released a breathy chuckle and slid her arms around his neck. She tilted her head, and her fingers played with his short hair. A teasing smile played at the corner of her mouth, and she wiggled her nose at him.

"I have to admit it was a bit of a surprise to wake up next to you. I honestly don't remember how I ended up there," she said.

"It was easier," he said.

"Easier, right...," she breathed, leaning up on her toes so her mouth was almost touching his. "I'm going to kiss you, Orion."

Orion's arms tightened around her waist. There was no way she could miss the evidence of his desire this close to his body. The feel of her hips pressing forward against him showed him that she was not only aware of it, but that she wasn't backing down. Her lips touched his, and all thought faded to pleasure.

Goddess, but I want this woman! he thought, opening his mouth for her when she teased his lips with her tongue.

Her arms tightened around his neck, and their kiss grew more frantic. Their breaths mixed together and their tongues dueled with each other, taking and giving. His hands slid down her back to her buttocks, and he cupped them. He lifted her up so that she could wrap her blue-clad legs around his waist like he had dreamed about last night.

Her fingers raked across his scalp, drawing a low moan from him. With her legs wrapped around him, he thrust his hips forward so that his arousal was pressed firmly against her. All he could think about was how much he wanted to rip the barrier of clothing away and bury his cock as deep as he could into her hot core. He wanted to lock them together and empty his hot seed deep into her womb.

She gasped, breaking the kiss. She continued to run tiny kisses over his face while rocking her hips back and forth against him. Her eyes were closed, and her lips parted as she sucked in tiny gasps of air. Her breathing increased along with the faster rotation of her hips.

Orion recognized that Jenny's arousal was building to a climax. He could feel the primitive desire to bring her pleasure grip him and he wanted to burn the memory of what she looked like when she came into his mind. Instinctively, he thrust his hips upward, leaning back slightly and bending his knees as she began rubbing against him faster.

"Ye… Oh, baby, yes… Yessssss!" she hissed out, bending forward to bite down on his shoulder as she came.

Orion closed his eyes and willed his body not to give in to his own desire. He was close to coming in his trousers like a lad. His knees grew weak when Jenny bit down on his shoulder in an effort to smother her cry. The only thing keeping them from falling to the ground was his threadbare determination not to disgrace himself in front of her.

He kept one arm under her ass and slid the other one up to press against her. If she rocked just once, he wasn't sure he would be able to keep his dignity. A shudder shook her, and she slowly released her grip on his shoulder to bury her face against his neck.

"I can't believe that happened. Why couldn't I have just self-combusted at the same time? I am so embarrassed," she whispered against his neck.

Orion softly chuckled. "You have nothing to be embarrassed about. I think of it as a very beautiful moment. I am also thankful you did not self-combust in my arms," he said.

She pulled back far enough to look at him with a raised eyebrow. "Why?" she asked.

"Because I want to see you come again and again," he said.

"But… What about you?" Jenny asked.

Orion grimaced and carefully lowered Jenny back to her feet. The muscle in his jaw twitched when she brushed against his cock. His body was still very much aroused.

"I thought perhaps it would be best for you to adjust to your new surroundings—and me—before we came together, though I would not oppose moving ahead of schedule," he explained.

"Oh… That is so sweet of you!" Jenny exclaimed, gazing up at him with an appreciative expression. "I think that is very noble."

"Father! Kelia has the food ready. Jenny, are you hungry?" Juno asked, running up to them.

"I thought I said we would be in shortly," Orion replied with a frown.

The smile on Juno's face faded, and the little boy came to a stop a few feet away. His shoulders drooped, and he rubbed the ground with his right foot. Orion wanted to groan at the dejected expression on Juno's face. His son knew he had a weakness for that sad look.

"I just remembered Jenny saying earlier that she was hungry. Dolph said it was part of our duties to take care of our mother. He found her, so she belongs to us, and we need to make sure we make her happy. I'm never happy if my stomach hurts," Juno said.

"I know exactly what you mean, Juno. Thank you for thinking about me and remembering that I said I was hungry," Jenny said, turning and bending over to hug the little boy.

Juno's face lit up, and Orion knew that his limited time alone with Jenny had come to an end. With a sigh of resignation, he motioned for Jenny and Juno to walk ahead of him. His stomach picked that moment to growl, sending Jenny and Juno into a fit of giggles.

One thing about having children, Orion thought as he followed the giggling pair down the path, *they are good at killing your desires—well, almost killing it.*

The last thought came when he saw Jenny shoot him a sympathetic smile over her shoulder. He gave her a rueful shrug in return. Once again, the responsibilities of family and the kingdom would come first—but it wouldn't always, and there would be times like a few minutes ago when he would make sure that he found himself alone with Jenny.

"A lot more," he muttered under his breath as he climbed the steps into the main part of the palace.

CHAPTER ELEVEN

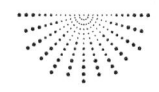

Several hours later, Jenny released a tired sigh. She was exhausted, confused, and still slightly mortified by her behavior earlier with Orion. Where on Earth had her lack of inhibitions come from she had no idea. She had intended a simple, pleasant kiss. Instead, she had heated up like a poker left in the fire until it was glowing red hot!

Granted, she wasn't a virgin, but she wasn't exactly a wild woman either. She'd had only two lovers in her life, one during her first year of college and the second shortly after she'd graduated. Neither had lasted. It was hard to have a long distance relationship, and they had quickly discovered they weren't interested in expending the effort to make it last. Jenny understood she was seeking someone to fill the emptiness in her life.

Before she knew what she really wanted in life, she'd had to find out what she didn't want first. She now knew she did not want a guy who needed a six pack of beer each night to make it through the day or one who thought leaving her behind while he went and had fun was okay. Granted, she never had the best examples of what a relationship should be like, but she'd always felt there was someone out there for her—someone who would make her feel loved, needed, appreciated and, well—that she was as important to him as he was to her.

Jenny jammed her hand into her pocket. She clutched the smooth stone she had found on the beach. She pulled it out and turned it over in her hand. It felt warm to the touch, probably from being in her pocket. The swirling colors reminded her of the stone that Orion had shown Magna. With a sigh, she slipped it back into her pocket and continued walking through the garden.

Orion was in a meeting, and the boys were playing with Kelia's grandchildren. Jenny had taken the opportunity to escape for some quiet time. She drew in a deep breath, not sure where to start to make sense of all her thoughts and emotions. Did she start with how she got here or her unexpected marriage or her physical and emotional reaction to Orion—a mythical creature living in a mythical world?

"I need therapy! Where is my life coach when I need her?" she groaned.

She lifted her hands to run them through her hair before she remembered that she had it in a ponytail. Pulling the band free, she shook out her long hair. She paused when she reached the end of the path and saw a vine covered door at the end of it. With another frustrated groan, she looked up at the crystal dome. Shafts of light shone down through the water from the sun above. Hundreds of tropical fish swam overhead, creating a myriad of dancing shadows.

She was about to give up on trying to solve all of her confused feelings and return to the palace when she heard the sound of voices on the other side of the wall. Biting her lip, she glanced back at the palace before walking over to the door. Lifting her hand, she brushed the vines aside. She blinked in surprise when she saw a small, square window in the door. Ornate bars covered it. It took a second to realize that the bars looked like coral and there were tiny fish decorating them.

Beyond the door, a truly magical world existed. The street, made of blocks of limestone, glowed white under the traffic. Jenny's mouth dropped open when she saw a cart go by, pulled by a creature that had the body of a seahorse but with four thick legs and webbed feet. Its tail swept back and forth like a whip. Jenny realized that this was the adult version of the small creatures in the cave when she'd first arrived here.

She instinctively reached up and unlatched the door when the creature moved out of sight. She pushed the door open and stepped out to see if she could still see it. Her eyes widened when she saw several men walking toward her carrying barrels on their shoulders. Jenny muttered a hasty apology and scooted out of the way. The heavy door slipped from her fingers and, before she could grab it, closed with a solid click.

"Oh, no," she muttered, reaching for the door.

There was no handle on the outside of the door. Jenny wrapped her hands on the bars and pulled, but the door wouldn't open. With a groan, she turned back around and glanced up and down the street. She would have to follow the palace wall until she found an entrance.

"Well, I wanted to see more of the world," she said.

Biting her lip, she looked both ways again before deciding to go to the left. It seemed like there was more traffic heading that way. It also looked like there were more shops in that direction. She wasn't opposed to doing a little browsing, even if she didn't have any money. It didn't cost anything to look.

It didn't take Jenny long to get lost in the beauty and fascination of this underwater world. She turned in a circle, staring in awe at the brightly decorated shops, the brilliantly colored sea dragons, and the wide variety of people strolling through the city. It was obvious that not everyone was from the Isle of the Sea Serpent—or at least she didn't think they were from the way they were dressed and their appearance.

"Is that a... oh, my!" Jenny breathed.

Across the street were two beings who could only have come from a mythical world. It was clear one was a man and the other was a woman, even though both of them were tall and muscular—and only had one eye in the center of their foreheads. They were animatedly talking to each other when a third person came up. This one looked surprisingly like a Minotaur. A shiver ran through Jenny when she remembered the tales she had read about these characters to her students.

A blush ran up her cheeks when the woman glanced up and caught her staring. Turning away, Jenny focused on the walkway in front of her for several feet before she glanced back over her shoulder. A frown creased her brow when she only saw the male Cyclops and the Minotaur man. Jenny turned back around and barely had time to stop before she ran into the missing woman. Dumbfounded, she looked up at the woman for a moment, unsure of what to say.

"Hi, I'm Jenny," she finally said with a slight squeak in her voice.

The woman's laugh made Jenny grimace. Now, that wasn't a very confident greeting. Placing her hands on her hips, she scowled at the woman.

"I'm Cyan. I like your hair. Where did you get that color?" the woman commented.

Jenny blinked in surprise and fingered a strand of her hair. "My dad's side of the family," she replied.

Cyan's lips drooped. "Hydra's heads, I had hoped it came from a dye," she said with a sigh.

Jenny glanced at Cyan's black hair. "You know, your hair would be really pretty with some red, purple, and pink or green along the ends. A teacher I worked with had a weekend job at a salon, and she was always leaving hair design books around the breakroom. I think if you got a tapered cut, it would really show off your face," she suggested.

"I think I am going to like you, Jenny," Cyan said with a grin.

"Well, that's better than wanting to step on me," Jenny retorted.

For added effect, Jenny wiped the back of her hand across her brow with an exaggerated sigh of fake relief. Cyan burst out laughing at

Jenny's teasing. Jenny couldn't help but grin back at the unusual woman.

"Boost, Meir, and I were on our way to get a drink, would you care to join us?" Cyan asked.

"I... Sure, why not? I have to tell you, this is all kind of new to me," Jenny shared.

"Is this your first time in the underwater city?" Cyan asked.

Jenny waited to reply until they crossed the street to meet up with Cyan's friends. She swallowed hard when the large woman stepped out in front of a cart. The two large sea dragons pulling it reared up on their hind legs. The driver growled a warning to Cyan who just grinned at the man and waved for Jenny to follow her.

"Yes... This is my first time here... in this world," Jenny said, stepping up onto the walkway.

"Who's your new friend, sweetheart?" Boost asked, brushing a kiss across Cyan's lips.

"A newcomer," Cyan replied.

"A newcomer. She looks different." The Minotaur bent forward and sniffed Jenny before straightening. "She smells funny, too."

"Meir, be nice," Cyan warned, shooting her friend a stern gaze.

"No offense. It isn't a bad smell," Meir said defensively.

"What kingdom are you from, Jenny?" Boost asked politely.

Jenny gazed at them as they paused to hear what she had to say. She wasn't sure if she should make something up or tell the truth. It wasn't likely they would know where Yachats or Portland was and she highly doubted that this world was going to invade the Earth if she told them where she came from. Heck, she didn't even know if it was possible to get back to her world anyway.

"Yachats, then Portland, but I still consider Yachats my hometown," Jenny replied.

Her statement was greeted with puzzled silence. Jenny watched as her new friends glanced at each other with confused expressions on their faces. Cyan shook her head at Boost, who shrugged.

"Never heard of that kingdom," Meir finally said, breaking the silence.

"We'll have to drink to this Yachats, then Portland hometown," Boost said.

"Sea Gully Tavern?" Cyan asked with a hopeful look.

"Of course," Boost replied.

Jenny wasn't sure what was happening, but she was swept along with the three strange but very nice mythical creatures that towered over her. She wondered what her friends and co-workers would say if they could see her now. Hell, she wished she could share this with her students. It would totally blow their minds *and* capture their attention faster than any video game.

"What is so funny?" Cyan asked, glancing down at Jenny.

"You'd never believe me if I told you," Jenny chuckled.

Cyan tilted her head and looked at Jenny with a curious expression. "Try me," she replied.

⁓

"Where is she?" Orion demanded.

"I ordered every available guard to search the palace and gardens," Coralus grimly replied.

"I've sent word to the isle guards here and above to search for her," Kapian stated.

"She said she was going for a walk in the garden. I saw her there earlier," Kelia added.

Orion lifted his hands and ran them through his hair. He should never have left her alone. What if the magic that brought her here took her away? What if Magna somehow returned and….

His mind refused to believe that Jenny had disappeared. His meeting with Kapian and the other officers of the realm had been interrupted by a long and detailed request from the Isle of the Pirates. Ashure was asking permission to race the sea stags and happened to mention at the end of the meeting that the Isle of the Elementals had vanished. Well, it did not necessarily vanish but, in Ashure's usual 'graceful' words, perhaps floated away due to all the hot air the King of the Elementals tended to blow. It was causing navigational issues with the currents. Ashure was hoping Orion could do something about that. Oh, and the pirate king hoped Orion would entertain the idea of selling his favorite stag, Sea Fire, for a reasonable price.

"Bloody pirate. I should have listened to Drago during the war and sent a tidal wave over the isle to wash all of them away," Orion muttered.

Orion closed his eyes and drew in a deep breath. He had used the momentary break to see if Jenny might like to explore the kingdom later this evening. That had been nearly an hour ago. He opened his eyes and stared back at Coralus and Kapian.

"Find her," he bit out.

"Your Majesty," a man said behind him.

Orion turned and watched a guard hurry toward him. He recognized the man as York, Shamill's former personal guard. The memory of the last time he spoke to the man flashed through his mind, and his stomach clenched. He waited impatiently for York to come to a stop.

"What is it?" Orion demanded.

"A vendor believes he saw the Queen slip through the gate at the end of the garden," York replied.

"Did he say which way she went?" Orion asked.

"Yes, Your Majesty. She was last seen walking toward the market. I've sent someone to inform the other guards and to inquire with the local merchants who may have seen which way she went," York added.

"Kelia, stay here. If Jenny returns…." His throat tightened.

"I will notify you the moment she returns," Kelia promised.

Orion silently cursed. The word 'if' struck him hard. The fact that Jenny was seen wandering along toward the market helped relieve some of his fear. He had forgotten about the door at the end of the garden. There was no way to re-enter once you walked out unless someone let you in. As a child, he had been locked out on more than one occasion when he slipped through it to escape Kelia in search of some great adventure.

Pushing past York, Orion strode through the open rotunda that connected the many sections of the palace and out through the covered patio to the gardens. Kapian, York, and Coralus followed closely behind him. He was almost at a run by the time he reached the door and pushed it open.

Pivoting to the left on the walkway, he began cutting through the crowd of merchants and patrons who parted when they saw him coming. His gaze swept over the heads, looking in vain for a glimmer of fire-coral red hair.

CHAPTER TWELVE

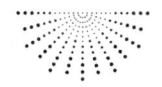

"You are saying this place you come from has carts that move by themselves?" Meir asked.

"The Isle of Magic and the Isle of the Elementals have carts that do that," Boost noted, lifting his tankard of beer to his lips.

"Yes, but they use magic or one of the elements to move them. She said her home's carts move mechanically," Cyan pointed out.

"Do you really have creatures that create lightning to power your airplanes—I mean, airships?" Jenny asked in awe.

"The Isle of the Monsters has some of the fastest airships in the Seven Kingdoms. Empress Nali can handle the thunderbirds better than anyone. She raises the chicks for all of our fleets," Boost explained.

"So, what exactly is a thunderbird?" Jenny asked in curiosity, sitting forward and resting her chin on her palm as she fiddled with the handle of the tankard of beer in front of her.

"A thunderbird has sleek blue-green feathers and several long, wispy tails that it snaps in the wind. You can hear the sound for miles. You know they are about to create a strong current when they do that. If you look closely, you will see the small bolts of lightning that interconnect them. It is always better to keep your distance when they are powering up. Each thunderbird has four translucent wings that fold back against their bodies," Cyan explained, drawing a vivid verbal picture of the flying power stations.

"I love how you can see the lines of electricity running through the veins in their wings," Meir added.

"You have to be careful around them even when they are not powered up. They have long, narrow heads and beaks filled with razor sharp teeth," Cyan said.

"Only the Cyclops are good at handling them. We can see the heat in their veins before anyone else," Boost interjected with a wink.

"Not only that, Cyclops only have one eye, so it is harder for the thunderbirds to pull them out," Meir chuckled.

"Ew! Are you serious?" Jenny asked, sitting back with an expression of distaste on her face.

"No, he is not serious," Cyan retorted. "They can pull one eye out just as easily as two or more."

"Okay, I'm staying away from the thunderbirds. If they don't fry you, they pick you apart," Jenny replied with a scrunching of her nose.

"Then cook you and eat you," Boost said with a nod.

Jenny was about to reply when a dark shadow passed overhead. She glanced up to see if it was a pod of whales. A frown creased her brow when she saw a dark shape spreading over the dome. It looked more like the ink of an octopus with the long tentacles radiating outward to cover the entire dome.

"Jenny!"

Jenny started in surprise when she heard her name called. Turning in her seat, she scanned the crowd of people who had stopped what they were doing to look up as well. Her gaze locked with Orion's.

"Orion! What are you doing here? I thought you were in meetings all day. Did you see the black stuff above the city? It looks like the ink of an octopus." Jenny said, standing up and pointing to the ceiling.

"Squid... and no ordinary one. This one can only be Architeuthis," Orion stated in a grim voice, wrapping his arm around her waist and pulling her close as he gazed up at the growing darkness.

"What is she doing out of the depths?" Coralus asked.

"She would not be here unless something disturbed her," Orion responded.

"The same for the Megatooth that attacked you," Kapian said.

"What did you see when you searched Magna's lair for the Eye of the Serpent, Kapian?" Orion asked.

"It was strange, the water was unusually cold and the bottom littered with dead and decaying creatures, but that isn't what surprised me," Kapian reluctantly admitted.

Jenny saw Orion turn his sharp gaze to the other man. A shiver ran through her at the troubled expression on Kapian's normally cheerful face. Kapian glanced at the two Cyclops and the Minotaur before his gaze swept over her face and settled back on Orion. Kapian's mouth tightened.

"What was it?" Orion asked in a quiet voice.

"The Eye of the Serpent was right where you suspected it would be. The cave was unprotected and the trident's gem lay on a small shelf with a collection of items. Some of the pieces were treasures from sunken ships, but mixed with them were things I remember Magna collecting when we were younger," Kapian said in a voice that sounded slightly haunted.

"You must be mistaken," Orion said with a wave of his hand.

"No. Remember the silver and ruby comb you bought from Ashure to give Magna for her birthday when you forgot and needed a gift?" Kapian reminded him.

"They weren't real rubies. They were polished glass that had been painted red. Ashure couldn't even be bothered with finding red glass to use," Orion retorted at the sting of being duped by the pirate.

Kapian nodded. "She had that, along with a tortoise shell clip that your mother gave her and the crystal globe I brought back from the Isle of the Elements that contained the ever-snow," Kapian insisted.

"If Magna is behind disturbing Architeuthis, then she will be close by. From what you've just said, there are some things that Magna still values. Perhaps we can use her sentimental attachment against her. Regardless of whether we can or not, we have to stop Architeuthis. It is a remote possibility, but Architeuthis may be strong enough to crack the dome over the city. The destruction would be devastating, even to those of us who can survive under the water," Orion grimly said, turning and pulling Jenny with him.

"But, what about everyone else? Cyan, Boost, and Meir? Can you evacuate the city?" Jenny asked anxiously as Orion pulled her behind him.

"No vessel can leave without risk of being attacked. Kapian, gather the elite guard. Coralus, secure the city and initiate emergency procedures. As soon as it is safe, begin evacuations to the surface," Orion ordered.

"What are you going to do?" Jenny asked.

Glancing from him to the dome with a mixture of awe and horror. She stumbled on the uneven pavement of limestone when she saw several long tentacles roll down along the center of the dome. She focused on where they were going so she wouldn't fall or hinder Orion.

They rounded a corner, and she saw the entrance to the palace. Even in their panic, people moved out of Orion's way as they ran past them. Out of the corner of her eye, she saw a woman clutch a little girl to her before fading before her eyes.

"Orion… that woman and child…," she gasped.

"They are Elementals," he replied as if that explained everything.

"Oh," was the only thing Jenny could think of as a response.

Picking up speed, she ran beside Orion as they passed through the gates. Kelia stood on the front steps with Dolph and Juno. They ran along the road leading to the steps. Jenny glanced over her shoulder when she felt the ground shake. She was half afraid the city was experiencing an earthquake on top of a colossal squid attack!

"Kelia, make sure that Jenny and the boys are in the emergency pod. Get them to the surface," Orion ordered.

"Yes, Your Majesty," Kelia said with a swift nod.

"What are you going to do, Orion?" Jenny asked, drawing in a deep breath.

Orion turned and cupped her face. He ran his thumb against her cheek. His eyes were dark and full of regret. Jenny's lips parted on a protest, but he bent forward and captured the words before she could voice them. Only when he had kissed her breathless did he release her and take several steps back.

"Keep her safe for me, Kelia," Orion said before turning and running toward the large red stag galloping toward him.

Jenny watched as he swung up onto the back of the stag as it passed by. Raising his hand in the air, he shouted a loud command. Jenny's lips parted when she saw a flash of light. When it faded, a trident like the one from the picture books she had read to her students was in his hand. More than a dozen men on sea dragons swept by where Kelia, the boys, and she were standing.

"Where are they going?" Jenny forced out despite the emotion threatening to choke her.

"His Majesty and his warriors will try to drive the creatures back to the depths of the ocean where they belong," Kelia said, bending to grip the boys' hands.

"What... What happens if they can't?" Jenny asked, glancing upward.

"Father will fight the creature," Juno said.

"Do not worry, Jenny. Father is very powerful. No one can defeat him as long as he has the trident," Dolph added.

"Yes, but...," Kelia started to say before she shook her head and turned away.

"But, what?" Jenny demanded, reaching a hand out to touch Kelia's arm.

Kelia looked up at the dome, then back at Jenny. "The trident is not at its full power. Orion and Kapian were able to retrieve one of the Eyes of the Sea Serpent, but the other is still lost. I can only pray to the Goddess that Magna has not found it," she said with a regretful shake of her head.

"What do the Eyes of the Sea Serpent do?" Jenny asked.

"They give the king the power over the sea and the creatures who live here. Only he can control the power," Kelia quietly replied.

Jenny was silent as she followed Kelia and the boys into the palace. She glanced up at the crystal dome when they passed through the rotunda. Her breath caught when she saw a flash of red as one of the tentacles rose off the clear ceiling. She stumbled when the squid struck the dome, causing the ground beneath her to tremble.

"Hurry! We must get to one of the escape pods," Kelia urged.

"I thought Father said that it would be too dangerous to use them until they could draw the creature away," Dolph said.

Kelia nodded. "Yes, but we will be safer inside one of them if the dome should crack. While we might be able to breath underwater, not everyone can," she reminded the boy.

"Like Jenny?" Juno asked.

Jenny caught Kelia's worried glance when the older woman looked over her shoulder. Neither of them said anything. Jenny bit her lip, thinking about Cyan, Boost, and Meir and the hundreds, if not thousands of other people who were like her.

"Coralus and the other warriors have trained for such an event. Most likely, the dome will hold. It has withstood many forces over the last thousand years," Kelia assured Jenny and the boys.

Jenny remained quiet. She was surprised when Kelia paused on the other side of the great rotunda. Kelia laid her hand on a panel near a golden door.

Glancing around, Jenny saw that there was a similar door in each of the twelve pillars that held up the curved arches of the rotunda. At first glance, the doors looked almost like the elevator doors back home, only these had clear windows in them. She had passed through the rotunda only once since her arrival and had been so fascinated by the openness of it that she hadn't paid close attention to the pillars.

"In you go," Kelia said, stepping to the side when the door slid open.

Jenny and Juno stepped into a small, clear, oval-shaped vessel. Juno quickly climbed up onto one of the seats and sat down. Jenny glanced around the escape vessel. The seats were lined up two by two with enough room for ten people.

The first two seats had controls, one that looked like the steering for an airplane and the other the toggle switches. The clear globe sat on two long tubes with propellers. Jenny was about to ask where she should sit when she heard Karin call out to Kelia.

"Grandmother!"

"Karin," Kelia said, her face tightening with concern when she saw her granddaughter struggling to carry one of her younger sisters. She hurried forward to help them. "What happened?"

"Mina fell down the stairs when the ground shook," Karin said.

"I sprained my ankle," Mina groaned.

"Dolph...," Kelia's voice died when the ground shook violently again.

Jenny had started forward to help Kelia and Karin when the dome shuddered again and a loud shriek rang throughout the underwater city. Jenny fell back against one of the seats and pressed her hands to her ears. Juno released a whimper and pulled his legs up in the seat with him. Out of the corner of her eye, she saw Dolph start to fall. He shot his hand out to steady himself and inadvertently touched the control panel. They all watched in horror as the door closed, sealing Jenny and Juno in the escape pod and Dolph and the others outside.

"No," Jenny gasped, throwing her hands out and pushing off the seat.

The loud screeching noise had stopped and a different sound surrounded them—this time of water gurgling. Jenny glanced out the front window of the escape pod and saw water pouring in around it. The moment the level reached the top of the two cylinders supporting it, a low hum started.

"Dolph! Open the door," Jenny cried out, trying to figure out a way to stop what was happening.

"Jenny!" Dolph yelled.

Jenny stumbled back when the escape pod began to float. She couldn't hear what Dolph and Kelia were saying. She frantically ran her hands over the panels next to the door but nothing happened. She reached out to steady herself when the locks holding the escape pod disengaged.

"Jenny, what do we do?" Juno asked, peeking up at her over his knees.

Turning, Jenny bit her lip and looked around. The console was beginning to flicker and light up. Weaving her way around the seats, she slid in front of the steering column.

The console looked pretty basic. There was a gauge that showed how much power the escape pod had, another gauge that gave depth, and one that showed the speed. There was also a separate screen that operated the lights and showed the oxygen levels.

Jenny pulled back on the steering wheel and released a soft, startled gasp when the escape pod tilted. She glanced at the floor where a single pedal stuck out. Looking at the depth gauge, she saw that the escape pod was beginning to rise.

"Juno, come up here and strap in," Jenny ordered, glancing over her shoulder at the little boy.

Juno nodded and slid out of his seat. He hurried to the molded seat next to her and climbed onto it. He grabbed the straps of the harness and quickly pulled them across his chest and waist, clicking them in place.

"I'm ready," Juno said.

"I wish I was," she muttered under her breath.

She gave Juno a wobbly smile before inhaling and releasing a long, calming breath. This couldn't be that much different than some of the boats she had driven. Heck, the controls looked more like a golf cart, and she had plenty of experience driving one of those after three summers working at the county golf course as a teenager.

The water pouring in was almost over the top of the escape pod by now. At the last minute, Jenny remembered she wasn't wearing a seat belt and fumbled for the straps on her seat. She clicked the last one into place less than a second before the escape pod shot upward at a stomach-dropping speed.

Swirls of water and bubbles surrounded them, making her feel like they were caught in a waterspout. Her stomach dropped back down to her feet when the jet of water pushing them up suddenly released them. A sense of disorientation swept through her and she blinked several times trying to see through the bubbles that were slowly spreading out.

"Jenny, watch out!" Juno cried.

Jenny reacted out of instinct, pressing her foot down on the pedal as far as it would go and pulled back on the steering wheel. The escape pod instantly responded, reversing with enough force that the two of them would have been thrown from their seats if not for the seat belts. She turned the steering wheel, and the escape pod veered to the left.

The dark tentacle that Juno had seen heading for them missed the escape pod by a mere foot. Seeing it up close and personal made Jenny realize how enormous the creature really was, and the fact that it wasn't alone. Nearly a dozen smaller versions of itself, if you could call creatures the size of a blue whale smaller, were battling with Orion's men.

Her eyes widened when she saw a flash of red swerve under a thick tentacle. From this distance, she could see the sharp, ivory mouth of the creature snapping. Horror filled her when she saw the struggling figure of one of the warriors and a blue sea dragon wrapped in the long, sludge gray tentacle. The squid was pulling both of them toward its mouth.

"Hang on," Jenny said, twisting the steering column hard to the right and flooring the escape pod.

"Watch out, there's a tentacle coming toward us from above," Juno warned.

"What do these levers do?" Jenny asked.

She nodded to the twin toggle levers. Juno leaned forward and grabbed them. He pulled them down and two arms shot out. A smile curved her lips when Juno emitted a short laugh of delight.

"We have arms too! If I push the button on top, they open and close like fingers," Juno laughed.

"Well, I say we kick some butt and save a merman and his sea dragon," Jenny said.

"I like that," Juno replied, grinning at Jenny.

Jenny glanced at him before refocusing on where she was going—which was away from those long, ugly, and dangerous tentacles. Spying a gap between the wiggling limbs, she pressed the steering wheel forward.

Jenny saw the warrior slice through the tentacle that had imprisoned him and finally break free. Architeuthis still held the sea dragon.

"The warrior is free, but the sea dragon isn't. You have to hurry, Jenny!" Juno said in an urgent voice.

Jenny's heart thundered in her chest as she weaved the small craft through the mass of tentacles that were larger and longer than some of the redwood trees back home.

"I'm going to come up under the tentacle. I want you to pick the crap out of it with those hands. Hopefully, it will release the sea dragon," Jenny instructed.

"I hope so, too," Juno agreed.

Jenny ignored the snapping claws of the mechanical arms. Kids were a natural when it came to video games. She would just have to trust that Juno would be able to clamp down and they could hold on long enough for the tentacle to uncoil and the sea dragon to get away.

Pressing the escape pod to go as fast as she could, Jenny swerved in an arc and came up from underneath. She maneuvered the escape pod so that it was between the sea dragon and the mouth of Architeuthis. Once she was close enough, Juno stretched the arms out and clamped both of the clawed hands around the feeding tentacle of the squid.

"Press the lever forward to put as much pressure on it as you can. I'm going to try to pull the arm back," she instructed.

"It's hard to hold on, Jenny," Juno complained.

"You have to, honey. We can do this," she said.

Personally, she wasn't so sure. The engines of the small pod were straining against the strength of the squid. She could hear the groaning of the metal arms. A flashing light, followed by an alarm sounded, but Jenny didn't have time to check what it was for.

Through the glass, she could see the tentacle starting to uncoil. The sea dragon that had stopped fighting a few minutes before must have felt the change as well because it began snapping its tail and pushing with its front legs again. Out of the darkness created by the ink, Jenny saw the warrior appear with a glowing sword. The man repeatedly struck at the squid's tentacle imprisoning the sea dragon. Bright red blood rose in a cloud and Jenny saw the tentacle unfurl like a rug rolling across the floor. The sea dragon kicked out and the warrior swung onto its back.

Jenny was about to tell Juno to release the clamps when the little boy squealed in terror. Out of the darkness, a smaller squid emerged. The creature struck the escape pod, ripping the arms from the vessel and sending it spiraling out of control.

A cry of dismay was ripped from Jenny as they spun around. Before their dizzy ride was finished, dark tentacles wrapped around them from behind and they were jerked down and away from where the main battle was going on. Jenny looked out through the front. In the growing distance, she could see Orion swinging the trident in his hand. A powerful funnel of water pushed back a line of squids trying to encircle him.

"There are too many of them," Jenny whispered.

"Father needs the full power of the trident. Dolph said that is the only way Father can control the creatures," Juno whimpered.

Jenny's lips parted as flashes of images suddenly merged together. She dropped her right hand to her side and rubbed the outside of her pocket. She felt the telltale lump of stone picked up on a beach far away in what felt like a lifetime ago.

"Juno, do you know what The Eye of the Sea Serpent looks like?" Jenny asked, reaching into her pocket and wrapping her fingers around the stone.

"Yes, it looks… It looks just like that," Juno replied. "How did you get the eye, Jenny?"

"Never mind that, we need to get it to your father," she said in a grim voice.

CHAPTER THIRTEEN

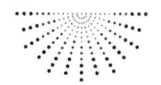

"Kapian, drive them away from the city," Orion shouted.

"We are down three warriors and five sea dragons," Kapian replied.

"Your Majesty, look!"

Orion turned to see an injured warrior on a bleeding sea dragon struggling to get to him. Both man and beast bore the wounds from the squid's suckers. Orion turned his gaze to follow where the man was pointing. One of the escape pods was barely visible through the turbulent and ink-stained water. Thick tentacles were wrapped around the vessel, pulling it down toward the edge and into the deeper water.

"We do not have enough men to spare to save them. We must choose between the lives of a few or the lives of thousands," Kapian said.

"It is the new Queen and your youngest son, Lord Orion. They fought to free my stag," the warrior said in a weary voice.

Despair hit Orion hard. Kapian was right—save the lives of two and risk the lives of thousands? As a ruler and a warrior, his duty was to his people and his kingdom… but, as a father and husband, his duty was to his family. Never before in his life had he been forced to make such a devastating choice.

"We draw Architeuthis away from the city. If she goes, the others will follow," Orion ordered in a thick voice, his gaze on the disappearing escape pod.

"Orion! I did not mean…," Kapian started to argue.

Orion turned his head and stared at his Captain of the Guard with eyes devoid of emotion. A chill had crept through him as he watched the squid slide over the edge of the precipice and sink down into the darkness along with his heart. With the responsibility of power and leadership also came sacrifice.

"NOW!" Orion snapped, pulling on the reins of his stag and turning toward the colossal squid. "Attack!"

~

"Juno, we have to get this stone to your father," Jenny said, frantically pressing the foot pedal.

The escape pod strained to break free before the lights began to flicker. Jenny's gaze swung down to the console. They were almost out of power.

"No, no, no, no, no!" Jenny groaned, leaning her head down until her forehead rested against her hands on the steering wheel.

"What's wrong? Why are the lights going out?" Juno asked.

Jenny lifted her head and looked out at the growing darkness. In the flickering light of the escape pod, she could see that they were descending along a long wall of rock. In frustration and rage, Jenny turned the steering wheel and pushed the pedal down one last time. Shock coursed through her when the escape pod suddenly rotated. The sound of a loud shriek echoed through the vessel. The tentacles holding them jerked for several minutes before falling away one by one.

"What just happened?" Jenny whispered.

She looked up through the top of the glass sphere with wide, confused eyes. The scraping of the suckers had etched deep grooves into the glass. The tentacle took its sweet time falling away.

Juno unhooked his seatbelt and climbed up on his seat to peer through the glass. Jenny undid her strap and cautiously stood up. She climbed up on her seat as well to see what was going on—and wished she hadn't when the eerie round eye of the squid stared lifelessly at her.

"I think you crushed it," Juno said, jumping on his seat to try to see more of the creature.

"I think I did more than that," Jenny replied.

When she rotated the escape pod, she did it at the perfect moment. Not only did it trap the squid between the escape pod and the cliff, but it happened at a point where the rocks protruded. From what she could see in the dimming glow of the outside lights, the creature's head was impaled on several long, sharp rocks.

"Uh-oh," Juno said when the last of the lights flickered.

Jenny looked down at the console. She climbed down off her chair and tried to press some of the buttons, hoping there was some kind of battery backup or emergency power. When nothing happened, she hit it with her fist.

"Ouch!" she muttered, rubbing her bruised hand.

"I don't think hitting it will make it work," Juno said, sliding down until he was sitting in his seat again.

"It's worked before, once or twice in the past, on a few things—my classroom stapler, the mouse that had been dropped a million times, my electric toothbrush. Never mind," Jenny muttered when she saw

Juno's confused expression. She sank down into the seat and stared moodily at the console. "I'll think of something."

"Father will come for us," Juno said.

Jenny could hear the uncertainty in Juno's voice. They had both seen the same situation up above. She leaned back in her seat and stared up at the darkness. A small red light was reflected in the glass, its glow cast by the emergency light. There was no telling how long it would last.

Jenny began to shiver as the cold started to sink in. Until that moment, she had forgotten that without power there would be no heat—or oxygen. Fear gripped her, and she closed her eyes against the burn of threatening tears. She had no idea how deep they were or how far they were from the city. It felt like they had fallen down forever. The fear grew when the escape pod made a strange creaking sound and shifted.

"Jenny, look!"

Juno's breathless whisper pulled her eyes open. Staring up at the glass ceiling, another reflected light had joined the red one. A confused frown creased her brow. She sat up and looked down at the floor. A soft, faint-green light with reds, yellows, and blues swirling inside glowed from the Eye of the Serpent. She must have dropped the stone without realizing it. Bending over, she picked it up. It felt warm in the palm of her hand. She closed her fingers around the stone and thought for a moment.

"Juno, can you breathe underwater like your father?" Jenny asked in a hesitant voice as an idea began to form in her head.

Juno started nodding his head. "Of course," he replied.

"If your dad had both Eyes of the Sea Serpent, could he send the squid away?" she asked, looking at the small boy.

"It would complete the trident. All sea creatures will listen to Father if he has the full power of the trident," Juno said in a confident voice.

"If… If there was a way out of the escape pod, could you take the Eye of the Sea Serpent to Orion... to your father? Could you do it without being caught by one of the squids?" Jenny demanded.

"I'm very small and very fast. The squid won't even see me," Juno replied.

Jenny could tell the little boy was getting excited. Was it right of her to ask such a small child to do something so dangerous? She stopped to debate the idea. If she didn't and they stayed in the escape pod together, they would both die from lack of oxygen. At least in the water, Juno had a chance of survival.

Shivers began to rack her body. Jenny didn't know if it was caused by the cold or fear—or a combination of the two. Juno was wearing less clothing, but he didn't appear to be affected by the cold the way she was. It made sense that if they lived under the water, their bodies would adjust to the thermoclines they were likely to experience.

"We need to find a way to get you out of here without flooding the escape pod," Jenny said, pushing up out of the seat.

"There is. Each year we must go through a training course. Father says it is to keep us... Well, he says something, but I just liked climbing in the escape pod and riding in it. This last time, Coralus took us, and he showed us how to get out if we needed to. Coralus is a lot more fun than Father. He let me drive and play with the arms. That is why I knew how to do it," Juno said with a grin.

"Can you show me what you need to do to get out?" Jenny asked.

Juno nodded and slid off his seat. Nearly ten minutes later, Jenny gave the boy the multi-colored stone and a huge hug. Tears burned her eyes, but she refused to let them fall. She must be brave for both of them at the moment.

"Your skin is like ice!" Juno said, rubbing his small hands up and down her arms.

"Ye... Yes, I'm a lit... little... co... cold. I... I need... you to... find... your father," Jenny forced out between her chattering teeth.

"I will. I'll bring him back. He will know how to fix the escape pod," Juno promised, sliding the Eye of the Serpent into the pocket of his pants.

Jenny watched the boy kick off his boots. All he wore were a pair of pants made out of the strange fabric and a vest. She was about to stand when he suddenly threw his arms around her neck and held onto her as tightly as his small arms could.

"I love you, Mother," Juno whispered.

Jenny buried her icy face against his neck for a moment, unable to speak. Leaning forward, she brushed a kiss across his cheek and stood up on trembling legs.

She walked with Juno toward the back of the escape pod. In an emergency, two hatches could be opened—one at the top and one at the bottom. She decided it would be safer to use the one on the bottom. She feared that a sudden shift in weight could cause the escape pod to become dislodged from the ledge where it was precariously perched along the cliffside.

Not to mention, it would be impossible for me to close the hatch with the water pouring in, she wearily thought.

Her hope was that the compressed air in the escape pod would prevent the water from coming in from the bottom, something like the air trapped in a diving bell. She bent over and pulled the locking mechanism. Drawing in a deep breath, she twisted the release handle and paused. She nodded to Juno that she was going to open the hatch.

"Are you ready?" she asked.

Juno nodded. "I'll be back," he promised.

"Be safe," Jenny said.

She turned the lever one more turn and pulled it open. The icy water that poured in around her ankles took her breath away. Juno held his arms by his side and stepped into the icy depths. The moment he was clear, Jenny did her best to close the hatch again. By the time she was able to get it sealed, the water was almost up to her knees.

"So... so... m...uch for the di...ving bell theor...y," she stuttered.

She reached out to steady herself when the escape pod groaned and began to move. Jenny grabbed the seat in front of her and pulled herself forward toward the front. In the distance, she could see a faint green glow moving further away from her. Juno was clear of the escape pod.

Jenny closed her eyes and slowly sank down in the pilot's seat when she felt, more than heard, the rocks giving way underneath the escape pod. The added weight of the water had done what she feared—shifted the escape pod. Her hands gripped the sides of her seat as the world tilted, and she felt the weightlessness under the escape pod again.

She swept past the remains of the squid. The escape pod bounced against more outcroppings of rocks, as it sank deeper along the ridge. Thrown from the seat, she tumbled to the back where she lay dazed in the rising water. One of the rocks must have hit the bottom hatch just right because the escape pod was beginning to flood again.

There was nothing Jenny could do until the wild ride ended. It happened faster than she'd expected. Her arms trembled as she pushed herself up off the floor. Wading through the water on frozen feet, she tried to seal the hatch again. A dark chunk of jagged rock about the size and thickness of a large tree trunk was jammed into the seal. No matter how hard she tried, she couldn't dislodge it.

Her fingers and legs numb from the cold, she waded back to the front and climbed up onto a seat. The water was coming in faster now. Jenny tried blowing on her hands to warm them up, but it was no use. Even her breath felt cold. She also noticed it was getting harder to breathe.

Pulling her knees up, she pressed them against her chest and wrapped her arms around her legs. She looked up through the top of the escape pod. Her breathing grew faster despite her attempts to remain calm. Her body was shivering so violently from the cold that she was amazed she didn't fall out of the seat. She whimpered when the water reached the edge of the seat and continued to rise.

Jenny unfolded her stiff legs and tried to push herself up. It took three times before she was able to stand on the seat. By the time she was able to do so, the water was up to her ankles.

"I don't want to die," Jenny said in a broken whisper. "Please, Orion… I don't want to die. I… want… to be… to be… a mom to… Dolph… and Jun… Juno. I wan… want to… be… I want to be… a wife… to you."

Jenny's sobs added to the shaking of her body. Lifting her hands up to press against the glass, she willed Orion to appear and save her. Surely she wasn't brought all this way to die a ghastly death in the dark, alone and frightened? If the Goddess had any mercy—any compassion—she would use some magic to save her from drowning. Yet, the water continued to rise, moving from her knees to her thighs to her waist, then her chest, and no magic creature came to save her.

When the water reached her chin, Jenny tilted her head back and gasped in the small sliver of space where there was still some air. Her mind and body had become blissfully numb from the cold. The only thing keeping her upright was the water surrounding her.

A choked sob escaped her when the last, precious pocket of air filled up. Closing her eyes, Jenny tried to concentrate on the meditation technique to slow her breathing. Memories of her life flashed through her mind.

She thought of Carly, wondering if she had fallen into this magical world only to die, and maybe that was the reason no one here knew of her. Painful regret for their short lives hit Jenny. She and Carly had so many dreams they had wanted to fulfill.

I found my merman, Carly. I hope you were able to find your dragon, even if it was for just a little while like me, Jenny prayed.

Her tears mixed with the salty water. Jenny focused on Orion's face. It was the only thing giving her a measure of comfort.

Finally, her burning lungs rebelled, and she drew in a gulp of water. Her body rejected it, struggling to expel the water and replace it with life-giving oxygen, to no avail. Each struggle brought more water into her starving lungs until there was no more air. Slowly, her body relaxed, and her eyes opened—blind to the darkness that surrounded her.

CHAPTER FOURTEEN

"What is it?" Drago asked in concern.

Carly sat trembling in their bed, tears streaming down her cheeks. She lifted a shaking hand to wipe them away when her mate sat up beside her. A choked sob escaped her and she turned into his warm arms and wrapped them around her.

"I had the worst dream ever," Carly choked out between ragged sobs.

"What was it about?" he asked.

Leaning back, Carly relaxed against Drago's warm body and rested her head against his chest. Like most dreams, she couldn't remember the details except the pain and sorrow—as if she had lost someone that she loved with all her heart.

"I need to check on the kids," Carly suddenly said.

She pulled away from Drago and threw the covers back. Sliding out of the massive bed, she reached for her robe and pulled it on. Drago quickly followed her, waving his hand so that a pair of loose-fitting trousers covered him.

"Was the dream about them? I will not let anything happen to them or you, Carly. Do you want me to kill someone? Maybe Ashure? No one would miss him very much. Did he cause you to have a bad dream?" Drago growled.

Carly released an exasperated sigh and giggled. "No, I don't want you to kill anyone—including Ashure. I don't know why everyone wants to do Ashure bodily harm. The guy wasn't *that* bad. The dream wasn't about the kids or me. It was about Jenny," she said, walking across the hallway to peer into their two sons' bedroom.

"Ah…," Drago said as he paused in the doorway behind her with a frown of confusion on his face. "I don't understand. If the dream was about Jenny, then why are you checking on the kids?"

Carly released a sigh. The boys must have had a pillow fight after she and Drago had gone to bed because their beds were destroyed again. Stone was sprawled out in his dragon form, his tail hanging off the side of the bed, and Drago Jr. was in his human form with his butt up in the air and a mountain of pillows surrounding him.

Neither boy had a bedspread on their bed. Those were currently the cover to their pirate fort. Carly frowned when she heard a soft snore coming from under the roof of the fort. Silently walking across the bedroom, she pulled the flap open and peered inside. Drago was right behind her, gazing over her shoulder.

Inside the fort was the newest addition to the family, Little Jenny. She was curled up on a pink blanket holding her stuffed dragon and sucking her thumb. Carly's expression softened at the sight. Her gaze moved to the large paper bird sleeping on the pillow next to her.

The enchanted bird raised its head and released a soft chirp. Carly placed a finger to her lips, and Big Knight nodded. From the new color on Big Knight's wings, it looked like Little Jenny had found the crayons that Carly had picked up and put away earlier.

"They are fine. I have the birds watching over them. If anyone or anything tries to harm them, the birds will let us know," Drago murmured near her ear.

"I know," Carly replied, pulling back and closing the entrance to the fort.

Drago helped her to her feet and they quietly returned to their bedroom. Carly walked across the room to where the open balcony doors. A light breeze blew in and she gazed out toward the ocean. She leaned against Drago when he wrapped his arms around her waist from behind and rested his chin on the top of her head.

"I wish I could remember the dream," Carly murmured.

"What do you remember?" Drago asked, bending and pressing a kiss to her temple.

Carly was silent for a moment before she released a long, sad sigh. She shook her head and placed her hands over Drago's. She couldn't remember anything but the residual feeling that was left behind—grief.

"I don't know. It felt like she was calling for help—then, I just felt such a tidal wave of sorrow—as if she was gone… for good," Carly replied, her voice thickening on the last two words.

"I am sure your friend is well. You have dreamed of her before," Drago said, turning her in his arms and lifting a hand to her chin.

"Yes, but never like this," Carly insisted.

"I wish there was a way to find your friend. If you like, I can approach the King and Queen of the Isle of Magic. They may know of a spell that could open the passage between our two worlds," Drago reluctantly offered.

Carly quickly shook her head. "No!" she said sharply before continuing in a softer voice. She ran her fingers along his chest, tangling them in his coarse hair. "No. We've talked about that before. Maybe before we had the kids, but not now. There is no way I will take a chance of returning to my world. What if I did and couldn't come back? I would be devastated to lose you and them."

Drago pulled Carly close against his body and held her like he would never let her go. Carly loved it when he held her like this. She wrapped her arms around his waist and hugged him back.

"Let's return to bed. The fear of losing you has made me horny," Drago stated.

Carly turned her face into his chest and giggled. That was another thing she loved about her mate, he knew how to say the most romantic things. Pulling back, she smiled up at him.

"I love you, Drago," she murmured.

"Show me how much," he replied.

Carly's smile turned wicked, and she slid her hand down to cup him. "Oh, boy. You are so going to know how much by the time I get done with you," she murmured.

She released him, sliding her hand along his full cock before she stepped away and untied her robe. She glanced over her shoulder and let it drop to the floor, keeping the belt in her hand. She shot him a heated look before her gown landed next to her robe.

"Goddess, woman. How did I get so lucky?" Drago muttered, waving his hand so that his trousers disappeared.

∽

In the darkness along the underwater cliff, Juno swam faster than he ever had before. His small body skimmed along the edge, weaving in and out of the rocks while he kept a keen eye out for any predators. His father, Kapian, and Coralus told him that a warrior always knew his surroundings and could feel the changes in the water.

Kicking upward, he slowed when he neared the top of the cliff. In the distance, he could see his father fighting the colossal squid. For a moment, he held onto the rock ledge and watched in awe.

His father swung the trident around and pierced a smaller squid with it. The squid lit up in a flash of brilliant green light. Juno could see its body glow and its veins highlighted before it writhed and crumbled to the ocean floor. The glow reminded Juno of the stone he was carrying.

Pulling himself upward, he pushed off the sand-covered rock bottom with his feet and stayed low, swimming as close to the bottom as he could, then headed in the direction of his father. Juno was halfway to where his father was fighting another squid when out of the corner of his eye he saw a black shadow rise to his right. Turning, he stared open-mouthed as the form took shape and Magna appeared.

"Go away! I don't like you," Juno exclaimed, swimming backwards several feet.

"I will call them away, but I can only do it for a few seconds, Juno. Tell Orion...." Magna winced and drew in a deep breath before she continued. "Tell your father... I'm sorry," she choked out as if in intense pain. "Go! I can only control them for a moment. Go, Juno, go!"

Juno twisted and kicked forward, trying to put as much distance as he could between himself and Magna. The squid between him and his father moved, giving him a narrow gap to pass through. He wanted to look over his shoulder to see if Magna was still there, but was afraid to. Passing through the floating tentacles of the colossal squid, Juno reached down into his pocket and wrapped his hand around the Eye of the Serpent. He was almost through when he felt a sharp pain in his lower leg, and he was jerked to a stop.

"Father! Help me!" Juno cried in terror and pain.

∼

Rage warred with agonizing grief. The first emotion Orion could handle, the second he couldn't. In an effort to push it deeper inside himself, he let the rage out, pouring all of his power into the battle.

He struck with a vengeance. Even without the trident, he would have been a deadly adversary. Although the trident didn't work without both of the Eyes of the Sea Serpent, he could still use it to channel his own magic.

Turning around, he pierced a squid that had come up behind him. The painful memory of Jenny and Juno helplessly being pulled down into the depths by one of the creatures flashed through his mind. His howl of rage chorused with the screech of the squid as it began to glow. Yanking the trident out of the dying creature, he turned when he heard a faint cry.

"Juno!" Orion whispered, his gaze frantically scanning the water for his son. "Juno!" he roared when he finally caught sight of him. "Kapian! Architeuthis has Juno!"

Orion pressed his heels into the side of Sea Fire and leaned forward. His heart raced as he weaved his way between the tentacles of two smaller squid trying to stop him. His eyes flashed with fire when he saw Magna on the other side of Architeuthis, her arms raised.

Lifting the trident in his hand, he focused his magic on her. The heat of his rage narrowed to a fine point on the center of Magna's chest where her black heart was beating. Orion whispered the words of a deadly spell, words he never would have spoken if not for the pain, grief, and rage pulsing through him. Sparks of red shot from the three tips of the trident, forming one powerful bolt.

Magna saw the bolt coming for her and continued to stand with her arms spread wide. Her black lips parted and her ghostly face held an accepting expression. A furious bellow escaped him when two of the squid darted in front of her at the last moment.

The red bolt of power hit and passed through the first squid before slamming into the second one. They both glowed a bright red before exploding with such force that the shockwave hit Architeuthis before rolling over Orion and his men. The shockwave stunned the colossal squid, and it released its hold on Juno.

Orion watched with horror as his son was tossed in the turbulent water before he silently sank down to the top of the dome covering the city below. Fighting to control Sea Fire, Orion kicked the sea dragon and guided him to where Juno lay unmoving. Kapian and the other men swiftly took advantage of Architeuthis' momentary disorientation to force the colossal squid away from the dome.

"Juno," Orion said.

Orion secured the trident to the saddle and slid off of Sea Fire. He turned and saw his small son lying on his side. He swam over to kneel next to Juno. Fearing that he had accomplished what Magna and the squid had tried to do, he tenderly reached out to touch Juno's small and fragile body. Orion's hands trembled when he gently turned his son toward him. Juno's lashes lay like crescents against his pale skin. Orion swallowed and brushed his hand along Juno's cheek.

"Father?" Juno murmured.

A chuckle of relief escaped Orion and he watched as Juno's lashes fluttered several times before the boy blinked up at him. He could see the confusion in his son's gaze. Pulling Juno up into his arms, Orion buried his face against his son's shoulder and rocked him for a moment before pulling back.

"Jenny...?" Orion asked, looking over toward the edge of the cliff.

Juno blinked up in confusion before his eyes cleared, and his lips parted. "She needs your help. The power went out in the escape pod. She crushed a squid with it," he rapidly explained, trying to push away from his father.

"She did what...? How did you get out of the escape pod?" Orion asked.

"Jenny opened the hatch. She said to give you this," Juno said, holding out his hand and opening his fingers to reveal the glowing stone in the middle of his palm.

"The eye... How... Where...?" Orion asked in shock, looking from the stone to Juno.

"Jenny had it. She said she found it on the beach before she followed Dolph," Juno explained. "Please, you have to help mother. Her hands were so cold. Please...."

Orion reached out and took the magical stone from Juno. Rising to his feet, he turned to Sea Fire and held out his hand. With a silent command, the trident rose from the saddle and soared through the water to his hand. Gripping the trident in his left hand, he opened his right hand to reveal the Eye of the Sea Serpent.

The stone glowed brightly in the dim light, the call of the trident beckoning it to return to its rightful place. The gem shot through the water, returning to the eye socket of the sea serpent. Power filled Orion, and his senses opened until he felt like he could touch every corner of the oceans.

"Return to your home, Architeuthis! I command these waters," Orion ordered, raising the trident above his head and swirling it around.

Funnels of water and energy flashed out of the forked weapon, hitting the squid and sending all of them far out into the ocean and away from the city. Orion ignored the triumphant shouts of his men. Instead, he focused his attention on where he last saw the escape pod with Jenny in it.

"Bring her to me," he ordered the water.

Three orbs of light burst from the tips of the trident. They swept outward, racing for the cliff to disappear over the edge. In the background, Orion heard Kapian give a quiet order for the uninjured to attend to the wounded warriors and sea dragons and return to the city.

"Juno, perhaps you should go...," Kapian started to say, but the little boy furiously shook his head.

"No, I will wait for mother. She might need me. Plus, I told her I would be very careful. This way she will know that I was," Juno said, standing closer to his father.

Orion's breath caught when he saw the first faint glow of light rising from the darkness. The orbs appeared first, followed by the escape pod, which was carried on a funnel of water. His gaze remained focused on the pod. He lowered the trident and pushed off the dome, swimming toward the pod where it settled on the sand to the west of the dome.

In the light of the orbs, he could see the glass was deeply etched from the squid's suckers. A relieved smile curved his lips when he saw Jenny raise her hand. The relief turned into confusion when her other hand rose as well. The movement was fluid. It wasn't until he drew closer that he could see her hair floating around her face like one of the ghostly images of an elemental.

"No!" Orion cried in horror.

The pod was filled with water! The realization of it hit him hard. The liquid that gave him and his people life had taken it from the beautiful woman he had claimed as his wife. His mind exploded in denial. Behind him, he could hear Kapian call out for Juno to stay back.

Sweeping the trident horizontally in front of him, the glass cracked and broke apart. Jenny's body floated forward and out of the escape pod. Orion's fingers loosened on the trident and he released it to pull Jenny into his arms. He gazed down into her pale, still face. Her lips were slightly parted, and her skin icy to his touch. He looked into her eyes and wanted to weep. There was no mischievous humor looking back at him—no fire, no desire. The brilliance of the colorful sea glass was gone—dimmed by the lack of fire that used to burn inside her.

His fingers tangled in her hair, and he pulled her against him. His body shook, and his mind felt like it was shattering. A sob caught in his throat and his body was wracked with violent shudders.

"No, she can't die. The Goddess said Jenny is our mother. She can't die," Juno sobbed, fighting to break free from Kapian. "The water showed Dolph where to find her."

"I'm so sorry," Orion whispered, running his hand over Jenny's hair.

"Orion...," Kapian said.

Orion looked at Kapian with tortured eyes. His friend had Juno in his arms. His youngest son was sobbing uncontrollably. Turning his gaze back to Kapian, he opened his mouth to speak before closing it and shaking his head.

"I will take him back to the palace," Kapian said.

Orion nodded and looked away. His heart wrenched when he heard Juno's cry of despair. Closing his eyes, he held Jenny tightly, unable to let her go. Only when he knew that they were alone did he allow the tears to fall. Gut-wrenching sobs shook his tall frame.

Sunlight from above streamed down through the now clear water surrounding them. The fish, that fled when Architeuthis and the other squid appeared, were returning. Life was returning to the underwater kingdom. Orion cried out in denial and tilted his head back to stare up at the flickering light from above.

No man should have to sacrifice so much or feel such pain, he thought.

He wanted to curse the Goddess for giving Jenny to him only to take her away. This beautiful woman had captured his heart and his imagination from the first moment he saw her. Drawing in a deep breath, he buried his face against her neck and pressed a kiss to her cold skin.

"Forgive me, Jenny. Please… forgive me for I don't think I will ever be able to forgive myself," he begged.

Orion slowly lifted his head and opened his eyes when he felt the brush of warm water swirling around him. His eyes widened when he saw the trident floating behind Jenny. The Eyes of the Sea Serpent were glowing in a brilliant swirl of colors. The trident's staff was shimmering with a radiant golden glow.

He gasped when bands of golden light reached out and wrapped around Jenny, pulling her from his arms. The protest on his lips died when a wave of warm, calming water swirled around him. Hope filled him when he saw the bands of light and a curtain of spiraling bubbles engulf Jenny's body.

The light from the trident danced across Jenny's skin, moving over her body like the ebbing tide against the soft sands. Her body glowed from within and the colors of the sea serpent's eyes began to absorb into her skin. Iridescent scales ran up her arms and along her neck and cheeks. Her shoes disappeared, and he watched in awe as her body twitched and her back bowed. Her arms floated upward. and her fingers spread. Thin webbing appeared between each digit. The same thing happened to her feet.

Her body stiffened as she drew in a deep breath through the thin narrow slits on each side of her neck. A stream of thin bubbles escaped her mouth when her lips parted. Her eyes that had been devoid of life just minutes before gazed upward. He could see her lashes flutter before she blinked several times. She stared up at the surface and the streams of light filtering through before her head slowly lowered and she gazed back at him with wide, confused eyes.

"Orion...," she whispered in uncertainty.

Orion slowly swam toward Jenny as the light and bubbles began to fade around her. He instinctively reached for her when she held her hands out in front of her and began to float upward. His hands slid along her arms as she studied the webbing between her fingers with a puzzled frown before she looked up at him again.

"Oh, Jenny. The Goddess has gifted me with my own beautiful mermaid," Orion said in a tender voice.

CHAPTER FIFTEEN

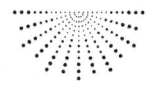

The sound of sobs pulled Jenny from the dazed confusion she was feeling. Orion slid off the back of his sea dragon and turned to help her down. She gazed down at him for a moment before she placed her hands on his shoulders.

They hadn't spoken since he swept her up onto the sea dragon and carried her back to the underwater city. Jenny had been in shock from her memories of drowning, and she was trying to understand what her mind was telling her about her transformation. Orion's arms tightened when he felt her shiver.

"Are you still cold?" he asked.

Jenny shook her head. No, she felt—good. She touched her arm with her hand. Her skin was warm to the touch and dry, thanks to the blast of air when they entered through the barrier tunnel that sealed the city from the water surrounding it. Several of the warriors turned when they entered, their eyes widening in shock when they saw Jenny.

"Who's crying? It sounds like Juno," Jenny said.

"He… He is very worried about you," Orion said.

Orion didn't go into the details of why Juno was upset—he didn't need to. Jenny already suspected that Juno must have seen her when she was...

No! I didn't die. I just... went to sleep for a little while—under the water—where there was no oxygen, Jenny decided.

"I died," she groaned.

"Yes," Orion replied.

Jenny stopped on the front steps leading into the palace. Her legs were trembling so much that she wasn't sure they would support her. Lifting a hand to smooth back the tangled hair from her face, she paused and looked at the webbing between her fingers.

"You could have lied," she whispered, staring at her hand.

"Never to you, Jenny. Besides, according to Kapian, Coralus, and Kelia, I'm not very good at it," Orion replied.

Jenny could feel her lips twitch in amusement. She opened and closed her hand several times to see if having the webbing made it feel different. Her toes curled on the smooth stone under her bare feet. A frown creased her brow.

"Where are my tennis shoes?" She asked, looking up at Orion.

Orion shrugged. "Somewhere in the ocean. I can search for your shoes if you are attached to them," he offered.

Jenny giggled and shook her head. "Now I know I'm dead! Who in real life would offer to search an entire ocean for a pair of tennis shoes?" she teased.

"I would, for you," Orion quietly replied, capturing her hand and lifting it to his lips.

"I think my legs will work now. It is breaking my heart to hear Juno so upset," Jenny said.

They both looked up when they heard footsteps hurrying toward them. Kapian and Coralus skidded to a stop outside the open doors. Kapian released a colorful curse while Coralus stared at Jenny in relief.

"You're alive," Kapian said.

Jenny burst out laughing at his incredulous, open-mouthed announcement. It would appear she wasn't the only one who was amazed by the fact. Gripping Orion's hand, she finished climbing the steps to the entrance.

"Yeah, and I've got webbed feet like a duck," Jenny replied. "Now, where are Juno and Dolph?"

Both Kapian and Coralus pointed inside. Jenny released Orion's hand and hurried past the two men who were standing with their mouths hanging open. Once she reassured the boys that she was fine, she would deal with everything that happened earlier, including more exploration of the physical changes to her body. Her lips lifted into an uncontrollable grin as she thought about what she could do now.

"Hot damn, I'm a real-life mermaid!" she breathed.

~

"She can't be gone. The water said she was the one," Dolph defiantly argued, glaring at Kelia and Karin.

Jenny's heart broke when she saw the older boy's red eyes and trembling chin. They were grouped together in the center of the rotunda. Kelia was holding Juno, who was noisily sobbing against her chest.

"I don't understand it either, Dolph. Let us return to your living quarters, and we can talk there," Kelia encouraged.

"I think that is a wonderful idea. Do you think we could get something to eat as well? I'm starving," Jenny said, slowly walking up to the group.

"You're not dead!" Juno exclaimed with a hiccup.

"No, I'm not… dead," Jenny chuckled, opening her arms to Juno when he hastily pulled away from Kelia and ran to her.

Jenny bent over and picked up Juno, holding the boy in her arms. Tears streamed down both of their faces as they held each other, laughing and crying, and hugging each other. Tears of happiness blurred her vision when Juno reached up and cupped her cheeks to look at her.

"I saw you…," Juno said, searching her face.

"I'm so proud of you, Juno. You were so brave," Jenny said, not wanting Juno to focus on what he had seen of her dead body.

"I swam faster than I ever swam before. I think I could've beat Dolph! Oh! I saw Magna. I told her to go away. She helped me get past the squids—squid—well, almost past them. One caught my leg, and then Father made this huge light, and it let me go. Kelia bandaged my leg so you can't see the marks right now, but…."

Juno was talking so fast that all Jenny could do was nod her head and make a few 'wow' comments. He still held her face between his hands, so she couldn't look over at the others. She drew in a deep breath when the little boy finally finished telling her what happened after he left the pod and wrapped his arms around her neck.

"I love you, Mother. I'm glad you aren't dead," Juno whispered in her ear.

"Mom. How about just calling me Mom? Mother is a bit formal for me. I love you, too, Juno," she said in a choked voice.

"Mom. I like that," Juno replied. "I think you should put me down now. I don't think warriors are supposed to be held."

"Warriors more than anyone need to be held," Orion said, stepping up behind them and placing his hand on Juno's back. "There is no shame in needing a hug, Juno. But… I do think you would get very heavy."

Juno lifted his head from Jenny's shoulder and grinned at his father. He held his arms out to Orion, and Jenny released him. She wiped at her damp cheeks, the tears starting again when she saw Orion's eyes briefly close with emotion as he held his son tightly in his arms. When he opened them again, she could see the flash of fear and the residual emotion of grief and despair in his eyes.

"Kelia, would you mind asking the chef to prepare a light meal for us?" Orion asked.

"With pleasure, Your Majesty," Kelia said, recognizing that Orion wanted some privacy with his family.

During the exchange, Jenny was quietly watching Dolph. The older boy was standing to the side, his head bowed. His shoulders were stiff and his fingers were clenched into fists. Walking over to him, Jenny knelt down and tenderly cupped his hands. She waited until he relaxed his fingers before she spoke.

"Thank you," she said.

Dolph refused to look at her. His fingers tightened on her hands, but all he did was maintain his rigid stance in front of her. Jenny waited. After several long seconds, Dolph drew in a shuddering breath.

"For what? It is my… my fault that… you…," he started to say before a soft sob escaped him.

"It wasn't your fault. What happened, happened for a reason," Jenny said, lifting a hand to wipe a tear from Dolph's cheek.

"You died," Dolph mumbled in a thick voice.

"Yes, and I awoke a mermaid," Jenny said with a soft chuckle. "If you had asked me if I thought that would happen today, I'd have said no," she teased.

A reluctant smile tugged at the corner of Dolph's mouth, and he quickly glanced at her face before looking down again. That brief look was enough for Jenny to know that she was making progress. She saw the glimmer of hope and curiosity in Dolph's eyes.

"What else?" he asked.

"What else? You ask what else?! Like being turned into a mermaid and being able to breathe underwater isn't awesome enough?" Jenny laughed.

"It is fun," Dolph agreed.

"Fun?! Are you kidding me? I've dreamed of being able to breathe underwater like a fish my whole life. Then, your brother fought off a legion of squid to find your dad who was battling this enormous beast with a mouth big enough to eat a hundred grown sea dragons and that had tentacles that went on for miles and miles," Jenny released a long, dramatic sigh. "The historians will be talking about this for *ages*!"

Juno giggled behind them. "Mom crushed one of the squids with the pod, Dolph," he said.

"You did?" Dolph asked, his eyes round with awe.

"Yes," Jenny replied, tapping his nose with the tip of her finger. "I sure did."

"It was gross. There were guts floating in the water," Juno added.

"Lots or just a little?" Dolph asked curiously.

Orion's rich laughter echoed through the rotunda. "Why don't we continue the graphic details of the demise of the bigger-than-legend squid after we have refreshments," he suggested.

Both boys eagerly nodded. Jenny stood up and waited for Orion to set down Juno. The two boys immediately began talking animatedly to each other—Dolph asking his brother questions, and Juno lavishly sharing his adventure. Jenny smiled at Orion when he slid his arm around her waist.

"What about the city? Shouldn't you be overseeing things and being—well, all kingly and such?" Jenny asked with a wave of her hand.

Orion released his grip on her waist to grab her hand. Threading his fingers through hers, he shook his head. Jenny's lips twitched at the mutinous expression on his face. The boys definitely got that look from their father.

"Kapian and Coralus can handle things. I have done my duty to my people today. Now I want to spend time with my family," he said in a serious tone.

"Family. I like the sound of that," Jenny softly admitted.

CHAPTER SIXTEEN

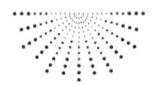

"Put your hand out and feel the water—listen to what it tells you," Orion gently instructed.

"Like this?" Jenny asked, spreading her fingers.

"Yes, what do your senses tell you?" Orion asked.

Jenny bit her lip and concentrated. She focused on processing the data she was receiving as the water flowed around her fingers and across the webbing between them. Her lips parted when she felt the vibration and a slight change in temperature.

"I feel a slight vibration… actually a bunch of them," she said before she paused and frowned. "But I also feel like there is something else—bigger. It feels almost like a wave rolling onto shore."

"Very good! Now, which direction?" Orion asked, swimming over to where she was floating.

Jenny slowly moved her hands back and forth. She felt like a living metal detector—waiting for the beep to tell her she was close, then moving back and forth in smaller and smaller sweeps until she found her treasure. When the vibrations felt the strongest, she stopped and pointed to the east. The other movement was a little more difficult to narrow in on. Each sensation came like a rolling wave breaking on a reef. She finally stopped and pointed to the north.

"Excellent. Keep your eyes open, and you will see what the vibrations are from," Orion said, wrapping his arms around her.

"This is like having built-in fiber optic Internet," Jenny joked, holding up her hands.

"I'm not sure what this fiber optic Internet is," Orion said with a frown.

"Orion, look!" Jenny whispered.

Swimming toward them was a school of small fish. Jenny's eyes lit up with delight when the vivid sky blue and silver fish circled around them. A juvenile paused in front of Jenny before darting forward. She giggled when the tiny fish nipped at her floating hair before trying to swim through it.

"Go on with you," Orion ordered in a firm voice.

Jenny's mouth didn't fall open this time like it had the first time Orion had ordered a sea creature to do something and it did. She grinned when the fish flicked its tail at Orion before swimming off to join the rest of the school.

"That's why there were so many vibrations in the water," she said, watching the school disappear.

"Yes," he said, turning her to the north.

Jenny's head fell back against his chest when she saw the dark shadow approaching from the north. Her hand wrapped around Orion's, and she pressed against him. She felt him press a kiss behind her ear.

"Watch," he murmured.

"I am," she muttered.

If Orion hadn't been holding her, Jenny would have bolted for the nearest rock to hide behind. That sense of unreality, which had been her constant companion since she arrived, swept through her once again, threatening to overwhelm her. Orion had sensed her confusion, especially since her transformation and had been incredibly patient with her as she adapted to all the changes in her body.

One of the not-so-surprising things she'd been dealing with was her growing feelings for Orion. While she loved his chivalry and protectiveness, she was ready for some serious, lets-get-the-sheets-dirty action. Over the past several weeks, she had learned that Orion was a master when it came to foreplay.

He would walk by her and leave a trailing touch that left her aching for more or give her a tender kiss when no one was looking. It was the heated looks and the promise in his eyes that almost destroyed her. After the one he gave her last night at dinner, she swore she wouldn't care who was in the room because there was going to be some serious R-rated paybacks.

Of course, it was the nights that hit her the hardest. Exhausted from her daily training sessions, she tried to stay awake in the massive bed that they shared. Invariably, she would fall asleep before he came to bed. She knew that he slept beside her because the pillow next to hers would show evidence of his presence and the sheets would still be warm with his scent. How he managed to slip out before she woke frustrated the hell out of her.

"Jenny, behold your wave-maker," Orion said.

A huge whale appeared out of the inky purple depths. It wasn't alone. Beside it, a calf about a quarter of its mother's size swam beside her. The only time Jenny had seen the creatures before was through the crystal dome of the city. She realized now that seeing them up close and personal was far different than viewing them from afar.

They were dark royal blue with a light blue underbelly. They looked very similar to the pictures she had seen of the blue whales except for the rows of fins along their backs, and these had back legs too. Jenny tilted her head back when the pair passed overhead, momentarily blocking the sunlight streaming down from above. A stream of bubbles escaped the breathing hole of the calf when it glanced down at them with curiosity, but it never slowed down. Jenny pulled free of Orion's arms and turned to watch them continue on their journey.

"They migrate this time of year, bringing their young back to the coves where they were born. The young ones will play in the cove while the mothers sun themselves on the beach. Those without young will begin their courtship," he explained.

Jenny was practically melting by the time he finished speaking. The fire was back in his eyes, this time hotter than ever—and they were alone for once. Unfortunately, they were also under the water.

Reaching out, she touched his check with her fingers, tenderly stroking his skin. Her body floated closer to his. A soft moan escaped her when he reached out and gripped her waist. His thumbs caressed her bare skin. The clothing that she wore was made of a material that allowed her to skim through the water. It also didn't absorb water, so it was dry when they emerged from it. The problem was that the majority of the outfits consisted of a vest and a pair of trousers for both men and women with the vest being optional for the men. Orion had opted out today.

"You are driving me crazy. You kiss me, touch me, sleep with me, but nothing else," she said, gazing into his eyes.

"I promised I would give you time, Jenny. Trust me, it has not been an easy promise to keep," Orion replied in a strained voice.

"Two days—okay, one—would have been enough," she said, leaning forward until her lips were almost touching his. "Maybe hours… I could have handled a couple of hours."

"You wait until now to tell me this…," Orion started to growl before she captured his lips and silenced him.

Now, it's my turn, Jenny thought as she threaded the fingers of one hand in his hair and followed a path toward the hard evidence of his arousal with the other.

Sizzling... that was what his nervous system was currently doing—melting from the heat that he had tried to contain since he'd first seen Jenny. He had done everything he could to behave, but he couldn't resist touching or kissing her when he passed by her.

The nights had been both bliss and torture. If he had been more noble, he would have given her the guest bedroom or even her own living quarters, but his desire for her kept him from those options

Unfortunately, holding her proved almost too much of a temptation for him, and he knew there was no way he would have been able to continue giving her the time he felt she needed to adjust.

In an effort to soothe his feelings of guilt at not being able to be separated from her, yet still find that balance, he had taken to training her with a ruthlessness he normally reserved for his personal warriors. He had worked her to the point of exhaustion each day.

The first few days, he had felt like a bastard. His punishing regimen had drawn disapproval from Kapian, Coralus, and Kelia, left his sons refusing to talk to him, and Jenny so tired that he had carried her to their rooms because she could barely stand. Kelia had snapped at him to leave Jenny alone, that he had done enough, and had taken Jenny under her protective wing the moment they returned each evening.

Kapian and Coralus both threatened to beat the shit out of him if he didn't stop. On the other hand, Jenny never complained or gave up. Each morning, she eagerly greeted him with a teasing smile and excited eyes that made him groan and feel even more like a heel.

Hearing the longing in her voice and the fact that he might have been torturing them both unnecessarily for weeks made him want to pull his hair out. His body, now fully inflamed and with nothing to stop it, was pulsing with anticipation. All thoughts of their first time together being tender and slow were quickly changing to hard, fast, and often. His mind reasoned that his body had weeks—if not years—to make up for. His body just wanted to make up for all of it right then and there.

Breaking the kiss, he held her tightly against him with his right arm. Raising his left arm, he snapped his fingers. Sea Fire, never far from them when they were away from the city, appeared out of the shadows. Orion turned, his arm still firmly around Jenny, and lifted her onto the stag.

"There is a cove above. We will have privacy there," he said.

"You mean, up there?" Jenny asked, glancing up at the surface.

"Yes. I'm feeling very selfish at the moment, and I have no desire to share you with anyone else," he said, pressing his heels against Sea Fire's sides.

"I like selfish. Selfish has its place in the world," Jenny said enthusiastically.

"Why did I not just tell you how much I wanted you weeks ago," he groaned.

Jenny laughed. "You are a little slow if you couldn't tell I wanted you when I had that meltdown in your arms," she pointed out, glancing over her shoulder.

"Witch, you would remind me of that when I'm ready to come like a stag on the hunt?" Orion retorted.

Jenny's response was to scoot back so that she could roll her hips. The feel of her soft buttocks against his swollen cock sent a mixture of pleasure and pain through him. He was so aroused that his ballsack felt like two stones covered by hard, crinkled flesh.

"Mm, I think this stag is ready to do some rutting," Jenny teasingly observed.

"Ah, my fire-haired mermaid, you drive me insane," he groaned.

He wasn't exaggerating either. The feel of her in his arms was driving him crazy. He urged Sea Fire to increase his speed and whispered to the water to send a current to help. Jenny's delighted laughter warmed his soul.

This is what it means to find your soulmate, he thought as they broke through the surface a few hundred yards from shore. This was a special place for him. A place where he'd come when he was younger to escape the responsibilities of his duties as the prince of his people and as an adult to deal with the responsibilities of being a king.

Sea Fire waded ashore. The stag's large feet sank into the silky white sand. Once on the beach, he reined the stag to a halt and dismounted. Reaching up, he helped Jenny down.

"Let me take care of Sea Fire. If you follow the trail, you'll find a treehouse where we will stay for the night. I used to come here often, but it has been a while since my last visit. I fear our accommodations may need a little work," Orion said.

Jenny glanced toward the path, then out over the small cove that opened out to the ocean. She turned to look at him. Orion caught himself staring at her hair. This was the first time he had seen it in the sunlight and he swore the strands glistened with fire.

"It is beautiful. I can see if there is anything I can do while you take care of Sea Fire," Jenny offered.

"Thank you. I will bring food for us as well," Orion said, finally giving in to the desire to touch her hair. "It changes color in the sunlight."

Laughing, Jenny stood on her toes and brushed a kiss across his lips. Her fingers teased the flesh of his stomach, and she looked at him with mischievous eyes. His hope of providing food and lodging first was fast losing out to saying to hell with everything else and taking care of their primitive desires. *Food and shelter are highly overrated at times like this,* he decided. He would have abandoned the stag, food, and the offer of a bed for the sand, sunshine, and Jenny, naked, if Sea Fire hadn't chosen that moment to push his head against Orion's lower back.

"I'll be waiting and ready," she promised before turning and walking across the sand toward the palm-lined path.

Orion reached up and scratched the stag under its chin when the beast placed his head on Orion's shoulder. They both watched Jenny until she disappeared. Releasing a long breath, Orion looked at the stag and shook his head.

"I am one very lucky man," Orion said to the stag.

The stag agreed with a loud snort. It was either an agreement that he was a lucky man or a reminder that he still hadn't taken off the bridle and saddle.

Drawing in a deep breath and releasing it, he set to work. The sooner he took care of the stag and found some food, the sooner he could focus on more enjoyable things—like all the wicked things he planned to do with Jenny.

CHAPTER SEVENTEEN

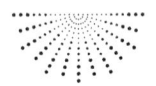

Streams of sunlight brightened the path while the cool breeze off the ocean and the shade of the trees made Jenny sure she had discovered a hidden paradise. The powdery white sand under her feet reminded her of the beaches along the Florida Panhandle. Spring Break never came fast enough after a long, cold winter.

The sound of water falling and birds singing made her think of the Swiss Family Robinson movie. Hopefully there wouldn't be a tiger or pirates joining them. Rounding a curve in the trail, Jenny stopped dead in her tracks. Raising her hand to her throat, she gazed in awe at the humble accommodations.

A massive tree that looked very similar to a Banyan or an Australian Cathedral Fig tree supported the hut. One of the teachers had gone to Australia and brought back some incredible photos of unusual trees with trunks wider than some houses which grew to astonishing heights. The tree's roots stretched from the limbs down into the ground, creating a curtain effect. Of course, the first thing Jenny thought about was how cool it would be to live in one.

"Hello, Mr. Robinson," Jenny murmured, stepping onto an elevated walkway that bridged a creek and continued upward, winding around the tree to reach the dwelling above.

Behind the tree, water flowed from a narrow waterfall that ended in a deep, clear pool before flowing into the stream that led out to the cove. Tropical plants in a wide variety, too many to count, grew along the rocks and the edge of the stream's banks. Flowers in every color under the sun dotted the landscape, while birds and insects buzzed from one to the other.

It was what was in the tree that drew Jenny's attention the most. The treehouse was not as elaborate as the one from the Robinson movie, but it was pretty damn close. Along with the winding walkway spiraling around the tree, a hut made out of the thin limbs, vines, and palm fronds was situated near the top of the tree, partially hidden by its thick branches.

Jenny slowly climbed the elevated walkway. Her hands caressed the woven rope railing as she walked. Her gaze followed several colorful birds as they flew up to sit on one of the window sills. As she reached the house, she was surprised to see thin, almost translucent netting covering the windows and doorways. Pushing the door panel aside, she entered.

The interior was an open room. She had discovered as she climbed up that the dwelling was built in a circle around the tree. From inside, she could see three hundred and sixty degrees.

The furnishings inside the hut were sparse. There was a primitive cooking area that consisted of a grill, a sink fed with water from the waterfall, several empty shelves, and a small round table with two chairs made from bent limbs and woven palm fronds. On the far side was the sleeping area. A vine-net was stretched out and fastened at each corner to form a hanging bed. On top of it was a mattress covered by a thick weatherproof tarp.

Jenny crossed over and folded the tarp. Protected by the tarp was a thin comforter and pillows. She looked around for a place to store the tarp. She discovered that the empty trunks scattered around the room were also used for seating. She opened one of the trunks and placed the tarp inside. Straightening, she gazed out over the treetops. She could see the beach and cove from here.

She smiled when she saw Sea Fire playing in the shallow water. Orion was stroking the sea dragon and feeding it fresh seaweed. Once the stag was finished, he patted the creature affectionately on the neck and waded deeper. He stood looking out at the ocean before his shoulders rolled, and he dove into the waves. Jenny's fingers curled along the polished wood. Her gaze skimmed the water searching for Orion.

Several minutes passed before he resurfaced. She understood what he was doing when he waded ashore and dropped a handful of long tubular stalks on a rock. He was gathering food for their dinner.

She watched him for several long minutes, admiring the sunlight on his tanned shoulders. His muscles rippled along his back when he turned to gaze out at the water again. Her eyes widened in appreciation when he bent over to pick up a shell. The form-fitting material of his trousers showcased his tight buttocks. Jenny's fingers itched to run her hands over that firm ass.

He must have felt her scrutiny because he turned and glanced in her direction. She wasn't sure if he could see her or not, but the idea began to form in her mind that she could surprise him with a romantic setting. She reluctantly turned her gaze away and glanced around the large room. It wasn't that dirty. The ultra-fine netting had protected the interior. A little dusting here and a sweep there and their accommodation would be fine.

She would finish exploring and cleaning the hut, then help find some food for their dinner. She had seen several varieties of fruit trees she recognized. She could pick some to go with their dinner.

First things first, though. She must do a quick inventory and clean up. Opening the trunks, she discovered extra bedding material, towels, and clothing. The sealed wooden containers did an excellent job of keeping everything clean. A short cabinet in the kitchen revealed the cleaning items she needed.

Jenny quickly set to work. She dampened a cloth and wiped down the polished wood counters in the kitchen and dusted the shelves. She retrieved dishes, cups, and utensils from one of the trunks and placed them on the shelf.

She discovered a unique feature between the bedroom and kitchen, the staircase to the bathroom! She had been wondering if there was one. She had also been curious as to why there was a railing along that single section of wall. Now she knew.

Curious, she descended the spiral staircase to the lower level. The bathroom took up the entire lower level. Jenny was impressed with the beautiful design and engineering it took to create the primitive, but very functional room. She would have to ask Orion how he was able to create plumbing that couldn't be seen.

Walking around the room, she saw a free-falling shower. She twisted the single knob and held her hand under the falling water. It was surprisingly warm to her touch. Of course, now that she had transformed, all water felt good, no matter the temperature. She twisted the knob again and turned off the water. Like the room above, this area was open with just the screening to protect it from the outside elements.

A toilet, sink, shelves, and another storage trunk filled with wood-scented towels finished off the room. She laughed when several small, brightly colored birds landed on the outside edge and peered in. Their orange, red, and purple feathers reminded her of some of the fish she had seen. Each one had a crest on its head that rose and fell when it chirped.

"Carly would have loved you guys. She was always a sucker for birds and dragons," Jenny informed them. "Ah, well, this isn't putting my plan to seduce Orion into action. Let's see if I can dazzle the clothes right off of him."

The birds chirped again, as if agreeing with her plan. Jenny laughed and took it as a good sign. She laid out some clean towels and the block of soap. Humming under her breath, she returned to the upper level, set the table and pulled the covers back on the bed.

"All night long... Mm, mm... All night long...," she sang.

She picked up a basket and danced down the spiral walkway, picking fruit that hung from the vines to go with their meal and flowers for the table. By the time she reached the bottom, her basket was overflowing. Placing it on a table near the walkway, she followed the stone path to the deep pool.

"I thought we could rinse the salt from our skin in the pool, or there is a shower up in the hut if you would prefer that," Orion said from behind her.

Jenny turned around in surprise. "Oh! I didn't hear you come up. I was going to...," she said before clamping her lips together.

"What were you going to do?" he asked.

Jenny's lips parted on a moan when she saw the fire burning in his eyes. She took a step toward him and reached out to touch him. All the weeks of longing suddenly came to a head. She wanted him—now.

"I was going to surprise you," she admitted.

"How?" he asked in a soft, seductive voice.

"By getting naked and jumping your bones. I hadn't thought much beyond that," she murmured, leaning into him. "I figured I'd see where it took me."

～

Orion groaned and captured Jenny's lips. She parted them and eagerly returned his kiss. Their tongues touched, dueling with each other in a primitive mating dance that heated their bodies to a fever pitch. Jenny's hand running over his chest, her nails lightly scraping against his skin, heightened his senses. He rocked his hips forward, pressing his thick cock against her. Pulling back, he ran his lips along her jaw.

"We'll try the shower later," he groaned against her neck.

"And the bed," Jenny said, releasing the fastenings of his trousers and pushing them down.

Orion deftly unbuttoned Jenny's vest. He pushed the material from her shoulders, following it with his lips. He loved the slight taste of salt against her skin. Cupping her breasts, he sucked on one of the taut nipples. His tongue rolled over the hard pebble before he nipped it.

"Oh, damn!" Jenny cried out.

Orion hissed when both of her hands wrapped around his cock, and she began stroking his throbbing length. He moved his hands down to her pants and quickly released the fastenings, pushing them down. The moment she was free of them, he lifted her up.

Her legs wrapped around his waist, reminding him of the last time he had held her like this. The difference this time was there was no barrier of clothing between them, just hot, aroused flesh. His cock was stiff, full, and straining. Any fear he had that Jenny wasn't ready for him was quickly alleviated when she rose up high enough for him to sink into her slick channel.

Orion locked his knees when he felt the tip of his cock against her liquid femininity. Her molten core was tight as it stretched around his sensitive head. She paused and gazed into his eyes.

"Don't let go of me," she instructed.

"Never," Orion promised in a voice thick with need.

His heart thundered at the triumphant smile curving her lips. She pulled back just far enough to stroke the head of his cock once more before sliding all the way down on his straining shaft, impaling herself as far as she could go. A shudder ran through him and he tightened his arms.

"Hold on to me," he ordered in a strained voice.

Jenny leaned against him, wrapping her arms tightly around his shoulders and pressed a kiss against his neck. Orion took a small step forward. If he didn't get into the water soon, they would both be on the hard path. He barely made it down the steps and into the pool. Now that his feet were planted against the ledge at the bottom of the steps, he relaxed his hold on Jenny and let the water help him.

His hands kneaded her buttocks, caressing them. She began to rock her hips, and she leaned back far enough that she could stretch her upper body to expose more of her breasts. Orion rocked his hips hard, squeezing the cheeks of her ass.

"You wanted to tease me," he said, thrusting into her.

"Yes," Jenny moaned.

"That can be very dangerous to a man who wants you as much as I do," Orion said, pulling back and thrusting again.

"It can? How dangerous?" Jenny asked, gripping his arms and gazing up at him.

"Very dangerous," Orion replied.

Jenny ran her hands up his arms, pulling herself close to him again. She threaded her fingers through his hair and gazed into his eyes. A mischievous smile curved her lips.

"I love danger," she retorted.

"Goddess, you will drive me over the edge," Orion muttered, capturing her lips.

Her confession and her teasing opened the floodgate inside Orion. Breaking the kiss, he gripped her hips and pulled out of her. Her loud hiss of protest soon turned to one of surprise when he turned her in his arms and gripped her wrists.

"Bend forward and brace your arms on the steps," he ordered.

Jenny swallowed and nodded. He gripped his throbbing cock in one hand and her hip with the other. The crystal clear water swirled around his thighs. With a soft order, two twirling bands of water wrapped around her wrists, holding her in place.

"What...?" Jenny gasped, startled.

"Water can be very playful," Orion murmured.

"I... Yes...," Jenny groaned, her head falling forward.

Jenny's broken groan died as he pushed into her again, this time from behind. He wanted her, every way, everywhere, with total abandon. Loving Jenny was nothing like the tame experiences he'd had in the past. Loving her was fierce, hot, and raw. Their coming together was primitive and powerful in need.

"You are mine, my beautiful mermaid," Orion cried out, feeling her warmth wrap around his cock.

Each movement brought painfully intense pleasure. Leaning forward, he cupped her breasts and pinched her nipples. His hips moved with agonizing precision as he pleasured her until she was pushing back against him with increasing need.

"Oh, baby. Oh, baby," her breathy chants increased until she stiffened and shuddered.

Orion felt her body tighten around his. Already stretched like a glove around his cock, her channel pulsed around him. He tensed as his body reacted to her orgasm, a long, drawn-out groan escaping him, and he shuddered as he emptied his hot seed into her womb—just like he had dreamed about for weeks.

"Release her," he ordered the water, before pulling her back against his body and falling backwards into the water.

They sank down, keeping their legs tangled in an attempt to keep them joined as long as possible. Floating under the water, Orion tenderly caressed Jenny's breasts. He could feel his body already anticipating their next joining.

"I love you, Jenny," he murmured, gazing up at the sunlight dancing through the water.

"Forever, my magical merman?" she asked, half-serious and half-teasing.

"Absolutely forever, my beautiful mermaid," Orion promised.

Jenny's body relaxed, wrapped in his strong embrace. Orion loved holding her tightly. She pressed back against him and moaned in disappointment when he eventually slid out of her. He tenderly turned her in his arms. Gazing at her, he drew her close once again and kissed her.

Drawing back, Jenny buried her face against his neck. "I love you, Orion. I never thought I could love someone the way I do you," she confessed.

Orion heard the faint uncertainty and fear in her voice. She had been hurt before, he was certain of that. The time they had together now would give her a chance to realize that he hadn't made his confession lightly. He loved her. She was everything he could wish for and more. She was his beautiful mermaid, and he would do everything he could to make sure she never had a reason to doubt his love.

~

They sat on the beach watching the sun slowly sink on the horizon. After their first round of lovemaking in the pool, they became famished. Too impatient to dress, they had used towels as temporary clothing.

Orion had grilled the sea mushrooms while Jenny washed and cut up the fruit. She giggled when Orion's towel kept coming loose. He had finally emitted a long expletive and tossed it aside. They barely made it through the meal before they tested out the hanging bed. Jenny discovered Orion liked her on top—and on the bottom and from behind and standing up and bending over.

In all honesty, she was amazed that she had the strength to walk down to the beach. She leaned her head against him and stared out at the fading light, thinking about how much her life had changed.

"Are you happy here, Jenny?" Orion asked.

Jenny sat up and looked at Orion in surprise. "Yes, very happy. Why?" she asked, trying to keep the self-doubt out of her voice.

Orion dug his toes into the sand. "I worry that you might miss your world. I have never asked if you had family—or someone else that you cared about," he confessed.

Jenny reached up and touched his cheek. This was the first time she had ever heard the sound of uncertainty in Orion's voice. He gazed back at her with a troubled expression.

"There was no one. Carly was really the only family I had. That is why it hurt so much when she disappeared. What about you? Are you happy?" she asked.

Orion reached out and gripped her hand, pulling it to his lips. Warmth filled her at the love shining from his eyes. Once again she was struck by the beauty of his features.

"More than I can ever show you, but I'm willing to try," he said.

"The shower?" she teased, laughing when he stood up and pulled her off the rock they'd been sitting on.

"I was thinking more of the beach," he said.

A soft gasp escaped Jenny when he pulled the thick towel off of her and laid it down. He placed his next to it, forming a bed over the warm sand. Gripping her hand, he twisted and pulled her down on top of him.

The warm, gentle breeze caressed her heated flesh as she sank down on Orion's thick cock. She rode him, slowly, tenderly as the stars began to shimmer up above, lighting their makeshift bed.

CHAPTER EIGHTEEN

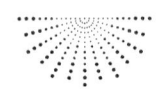

"I thought I would find you here," Kapian said, walking out of the water.

"I sent a message," Orion grunted, refocusing his attention on the rope he was weaving.

"You said 'I won't be back for a few days. Don't worry and don't come. Tell the boys to behave until I get back.' That is hardly a message. It is very cryptic," Kapian dryly stated.

Orion glanced up again with a frown. "What have they done now?"

"Who? Oh, the boys? Nothing. Well, almost nothing. Juno has been driving Kelia crazy with questions about the baby, like what color his baby sister's room should be and whether she should stay in his and Dolph's room so they can protect her better. Other than that, they have been surprisingly mellow for a change," Kapian replied.

Orion grunted again when Kapian sat down beside him. It would appear his anti-social behavior was not going to drive off his friend. Glancing over his shoulder, Orion hoped that Jenny was aware that they were no longer alone. The last few days had been blissful—and relatively clothes-free.

He had pulled on a pair of trousers earlier so he could take care of Sea Fire and harvest more food. He'd been heading back when he felt Kapian's approach and decided it would be best to wait for his friend. A deep sigh escaped him. It would appear life and responsibilities were about to intrude on their 'honeymoon' as she called their time alone.

"If the boys have not destroyed the kingdom, disappeared, or created some other type of havoc, what could possibly be so dire that you couldn't wait a few more days?" Orion asked.

Kapian chuckled before he grew serious. "The Queen of the Isle of Magic wishes to speak with you—in person," he said.

Orion frowned. "I can meet with her at the palace on the surface," he said, rising to his feet.

Kapian shook his head. "She has asked that you journey to Magic. She says it is imperative that she remain on the isle," he said.

"What is going on? First the Elementals disappear, then the Queen of Magic wishes for me to present myself to her. I have not seen either in almost a decade. I have enough on my hands with my own kingdom!" Orion retorted, standing.

Kapian looked back at him with a grim expression. "I fear it has to do with your cousin," he admitted with a grimace of distaste.

"Magna. My father should have struck her dead instead of just banishing her. It would have prevented the continuing misery that she unleashes!" Orion bit out in frustration.

Kapian nodded in agreement. Staring out at the ocean, Orion couldn't help but think of his cousin. The three of them had spent many a day—and night—on this beach dreaming of their plans for the future and plotting ways to change Orion's. The last time they'd been here was the night he and Magna had seen the meteorite flashing through the night. They had raced out to retrieve it.

Orion didn't remember much of that night. Something had spooked his sea dragon, and he had struck his head. It wasn't long after that night that he'd noticed a change in Magna and an end to the friendship that had been created out of love, laughter, and dreams.

"We will return within the hour. Prepare to leave later this afternoon," Orion stated.

"I'll ready the members of the elite guard," Kapian said, walking back toward the water.

Orion nodded. "Kapian...."

Kapian turned. "Yes, my friend?"

"I want you to know the shower idea was a good one," Orion replied with a wry grin.

Kapian groaned and shook his head. "Now I will have an image of you stuck in my head that I never wanted to see," he groaned.

Orion's laughter followed Kapian as he dove back into the water and swam over to where his stag was playing with Sea Fire. Orion didn't move until he knew Kapian was gone. With a sigh, he turned back toward the hut. It looked like the honeymoon was over.

∽

"Listen carefully to what Kelia tells you and don't give her any trouble. Promise?" Jenny asked.

"We promise. When you come back, will you please bring our sister with you?" Juno asked.

Jenny resisted the urge to roll her eyes. Juno was one of the most single-minded, persistent little boys she had ever met—and she had met a lot of them! When he'd heard that they had returned, he had come running out with a yell of excitement. He had swept past his dad's open arms and straight to her.

"So, do you have her? Is she still in your stomach?" he had asked, pressing his ear against her. "I don't hear anything."

Jenny choked back her laughter even as everyone around them chuckled and started ribbing Orion. Juno had been heartbroken when Jenny carefully explained that even *if* she had a baby sister in the oven, it would take months before the baby would be ready to visit. That would have been fine except for Juno's precious response when he turned his determined gaze to his father.

"You need to keep father busy if it is going to take months to make her," Juno informed her.

Jenny didn't correct Juno's misunderstanding of how his baby sister would be made. Instead, she leaned forward, pressed a kiss to Juno's cheek, and told him she would do her very best to make sure that she kept his dad busy. She had to admit, the idea was beginning to grow on her—especially the part about keeping Orion busy. She glanced up at Orion to see how he was handling her conversation with Juno. The heated look in his eyes made her think of other things that turned her cheeks a nice rosy shade of red.

~

They had been on their journey for nearly two hours before Orion reined in Sea Fire to swim near Jenny who was riding her new sea dragon, Sea Star. She hadn't minded. Orion and Kapian were discussing a wide range of issues, most of which she didn't understand. Before long, one of the guards named York had struck up a conversation with her, answering the questions she had about her sea dragon, the Isle of Magic, and how long it would take.

"York," Orion nodded, dismissing the guard with a curt nod of his head.

"Your Majesty," York politely replied, reining his sea stag in behind them a fair distance to give them privacy.

"Ouch," she said in a quiet voice.

Orion turned his head to look at her with a frown. "You are hurt?" he asked.

Jenny shook her head. "No, but I think York is feeling the effects of the freezer burn you just gave him," she reflected.

Orion turned to face forward. Jenny could see the muscle twitching in his jaw. Reining Sea Star closer, she reached out and touched Orion's arm.

"What is it?" she asked.

She could feel the muscles tense before they relaxed under her concerned touch. It was obvious that there was a history between the two men, but she couldn't fathom what it could be to have upset Orion so badly. Every time she had seen the guard at the palace, he had been very polite and attentive.

"York was Shamill's personal guard," Orion stated in a tight voice.

"Oh," Jenny replied, unsure of what else to say.

"It would appear he was very personal," Orion added.

"Oh! I... Kelia said that Shamill died after Juno was born," Jenny said.

"Kapian and I had been out at sea when we felt a minor earthquake. Concerned, we hurriedly returned to the Isle of the Sea Serpent. There had been some minor damage to the older buildings, but nothing serious—or so I thought. York approached me to tell me that Shamill had been injured. She had been in poor health off and on throughout her pregnancy with Juno. That and her fear of heights made it highly unlikely that she would have been walking along the upper paths near the cliffs. Shamill was deathly afraid of heights to the point where she would not even climb the stairs to the second floor," he told her.

"Oh my god, she didn't fall off the cliff did she?" Jenny asked in horror.

Orion shook his head. "No, part of the wall along the path collapsed. Her injuries thrust her into early labor. The injuries, her already weakened health, and giving birth to Juno were too much. She died shortly after the birth," he shared.

"How did you know…? Are you sure they were, you know, friendly?" she asked.

Orion glanced at her and nodded. "Shamill was on her way to see York. I found copies of letters among Shamill's belongings. She was trying to find a way to break off their affair. It would appear her love for her children outweighed her love for him," he bitterly retorted.

"I can't imagine loving someone and finding out they had betrayed me like that. It is especially difficult if there is no closure for understanding why," she said.

"I didn't love her, nor she me. At least not the way I love you. We were friends. Our marriage was arranged by our parents out of fear of what Magna might do next," he admitted.

"An arranged marriage? Okay, I'm putting my foot down, here and now, so that we are on the same page—our kids get to make their own choices. If they screw up, that is up to them to live and learn," she said with a wave of her hand.

Orion chuckled and nodded. "I think I have done the live and learn lesson. Our children will make their own choices," he agreed.

"You bet your ass they will," she giggled when he grabbed her hand and pulled her off of Sea Star and onto his lap.

There were some serious advantages to living under the water, she thought as he bent his head to kiss her.

CHAPTER NINETEEN

Jenny watched Orion and Kapian slowly emerge out of the crystal clear waters of the lagoon. Sea Fire's dark red body glistened in the bright sunlight. Kapian's black sea dragon shook its head nervously and pranced to the side several feet, splashing water up around it. On the beach stood a dozen waiting soldiers.

A tall young man stepped forward and stood unsmiling before Orion and Kapian before speaking. He turned his attention to Orion and bowed his head. They spoke for several minutes before the man turned and motioned with his hand.

Jenny was surprised when the guards parted and an elegant older woman stepped forward. The woman waved her hand and the sand shifted, becoming a solid surface. Jenny started when Sea Star tossed her head and began moving toward the beach. She tried to pull back on the reins, but the reins disappeared.

"What the…?" she exclaimed.

Jenny gripped the front of the saddle when Sea Star waded out of the water and stopped next to Orion. She had to hand it to Orion, he didn't turn in her direction or even appear to blink at what had happened. Jenny swallowed when the soldiers fanned out behind the woman. Each of them was wearing full armor, some holding swords, some holding spears, and some holding bows.

"Sea King," the woman said.

"Greetings Queen Magika," Orion replied with a bow of his head.

The woman's gaze turned to Jenny. They studied each other; the older woman's eyes were filled with curiosity while Jenny was pretty sure hers were filled with a 'what-the-fuck' expression. A hint of a smile curved the corners of the woman's lips.

"It is times like this that I wish the Goddess would have gifted us her mirror instead of her magic," Magika said, looking back at Orion.

"I'm sure Nali has often wished she had been given the gift of your magic instead of a mirror and an isle full of monsters," Orion dryly replied.

Magika studied Orion for several seconds before she nodded and smiled. "Yes, I imagine you are correct. Please, sit with me," the Queen replied with a wave of her hand.

Jenny drew in a hissing breath when three chairs, a table, and refreshments appeared under a large open-air tent. Orion dismounted from Sea Fire and turned to help Jenny down from her mount. She was surprised when Kapian pulled his stag back and led the other stags a short distance away before he dismounted and stood near them.

Jenny swore she could see the tension in the air between the young warrior and Kapian as their respective rulers walked away. She instinctively reached for Orion's hand before thinking maybe this isn't what royalty should do. Biting her lip, she started to pull her hand away but Orion wouldn't release it. Instead, he squeezed it in reassurance.

"If you don't mind, I would like to ask if the King will be joining us," Orion inquired.

"The King is… unwell at the moment," the Queen hesitantly replied.

"My sincere apologies. I hope the King feels better soon," Orion replied.

The Queen looked at Orion. Her expression was serious—and very cautious. She studied his face for several seconds before she waved her hand to the chairs facing her. She sat down and patiently waited for Jenny and Orion to do the same before she spoke again.

"Tell me of the magic your cousin uses," Magika asked.

Jenny listened as Orion and the Queen talked. Her eyes, though, followed the enchanted dishes. The tea pot lifted in the air and floated over to the cups. After filling them, it returned to the silver tray. A cup with four tiny feet and with what looked like sugar cubes in it walked over to the Queen's cup and added two cubes before moving to Jenny's cup. The handle picked up a cube and held it up. Jenny shook her head and smiled.

"No, thank you," she said.

The handle replaced the cube and moved to Orion's cup. He waved his hand at the cup in dismissal. The cup scurried back to the tray and hid behind the teapot. Jenny couldn't help but wonder if some of the famous writers of fairy tales might have come to this world during their lifetimes.

"It would certainly explain a lot," she mused out loud.

"Explain what?" the Queen asked.

Jenny bent forward and picked up her cup. She studied it for a few seconds before looking back at the Queen. A wry smile curved her lips. She hadn't realized that she had spoken aloud.

"I was just wondering if Gabrielle-Suzanne Barbot de Villeneuve, Charles Perrault, or The Brothers Grimm had ever visited your world," Jenny said.

The Queen's expression grew thoughtful before she shook her head. "I have never heard of anyone by those names," the Queen finally replied.

"What about a woman named Carly?" Jenny impulsively asked.

Once again the Queen's expression grew thoughtful. She frowned and looked to the young warrior who stood off to the side. Within seconds, he was standing next to her.

"Yes, Your Majesty," the man said.

"Isha, have you heard of a woman named Carly?" Magika asked.

Isha frowned. He glanced at Jenny before returning his gaze to the Queen. He shook his head.

"Nay, Your Majesty, but I have heard it said that Drago has taken a mate. It is said the woman came from a distant realm," he continued.

"Drago?" Jenny asked, turning to look at Orion.

"The Dragon King," Orion replied.

~

Orion opened the flap of the tent he and Jenny had been given. The Queen had been adamant that it would be best if they remained on the beach. Suspicious, he had instructed Kapian to send two scouts out to patrol the waters.

"She is hiding something," Kapian insisted.

"I agree," Orion replied.

"Why would she insist that you come all this way just to have tea and chat about Magna's magic?" Kapian asked, puzzled.

Orion shrugged. "If anyone should be asking about Magna's magic, it is I who should be. My cousin's mother was from this kingdom while her father was from the sea. Magika must be aware of that," he reflected.

"Your Majesty, a guard approaches," one of Orion's guards warned.

Kapian raised his eyebrow at Orion before he walked over and pulled aside the flap of the tent. Orion stood and watched from the entrance as Isha strode toward them. The young warrior slowed to a stop when he saw Orion watching him.

"With your permission, Sea King, I would like a moment to have a word with you," Isha said in a stiff voice.

Kapian glanced at Orion, who nodded. "Come in," Kapian ordered.

Isha shot Kapian a cold look before stepping through the entrance to the tent. The warrior turned and waited for Kapian to close the tent flap before he returned his attention to Orion. The slight hesitation or the fact that he did not speak until the flap had sealed did not go unnoticed by Orion.

"What is it?" Orion demanded, folding his arms across his chest.

"The tents have been spelled so that what is said outside can be heard, but what is said inside cannot as a precaution," Isha explained.

"That still doesn't tell us what is going on," Kapian bluntly stated.

Isha's mouth tightened at Kapian's tone. Orion had to give the young warrior credit for not reacting otherwise. Kapian was skilled at baiting his adversaries into revealing information in a moment of anger.

"The Queen wished to meet with you to assess whether or not you sent Magna to steal the Sword of the Goddess," Isha replied.

"All the rulers know of the devastation that stealing another realm's gift could bring, and Magna's betrayal is no secret. Why would anyone allow her an audience, much less anywhere near their kingdoms?" Orion asked.

Isha pursed his lips and shook his head. "I will share the facts I know, Your Majesty. We know that Magna instigated the wars between the isles, and we know that she is responsible for what happened to the dragons," Isha began.

"Can you tell us something we don't already know?" Kapian asked with a sardonic twist to his lips.

Isha shot Kapian a heated glare. "All magic is unique. It has its own fingerprint, specific to each individual. Each of our magic skills are also different. Some individuals make excellent warriors, while others may be healers or farmers. The magic defines who we are and that does not alter," he explained.

"That is all fine and good, but what does that have to do with Magna?" Orion asked.

Isha turned to look at Orion. "Her magic has changed. What it is now is unlike anything the Queen has ever seen before. Nearly a fortnight ago, the Queen entered the royal study to speak with the King. His Majesty was standing near the window holding a black box. When the Queen asked about it, the King reacted—harshly," Isha said.

"What was in the box, and where did he get it?" Orion asked, still unsure where this was leading.

"At first, the King was very protective of the box—caressing it and muttering under his breath. In time, he revealed it had been a gift from Magna. The King told Her Majesty that Magna had briefly appeared before him in the study to ask forgiveness for what she had done. She offered him the box as a token of her sincerity," Isha shared with a troubled expression. "The Queen knew the feel of Magna's magic, and she was concerned. The magic she had felt in the study was tainted somehow and unlike the magic's signature she remembered. Her Majesty said that while there was a faint residue of Magna in it, there was very little of the magic she knew from Magna's visits to the palace with her parents when she was younger. When the Queen asked to hold the box to examine it, the King again became extremely agitated. Out of concern, Her Majesty insisted that the King share the box according to the Law of Balance. The magic that binds them prevented the King from refusing the Queen's request. When the King went to retrieve the box, it was gone. The Queen found him after he collapsed on the floor of the study."

"Do your healers know what happened to him?" Kapian asked.

Isha shook his head. "He is recovering, but it has taken time and the

Queen is afraid to be away from his side for long. Her Majesty believes that whatever magic Magna has will only grow more powerful if she is not stopped. Magna was able to use her magic on the dragons because she took them by surprise. No one expected magic on this scale. The Queen has sworn to do everything she can to learn the source of Magna's magic, but she needs your help in capturing the Sea Witch," he quietly stated.

"What of Magna's parents? They live on the Isle of Magic. Has she contacted them?" he asked.

"No, I have two of my best trackers monitoring their home," Isha grimly replied.

Orion nodded. "Give Queen Magika my pledge to do all I can to find Magna and stop her. We will be leaving at first light," he said.

Isha sharply bowed his head and turned. Kapian opened the flap of the tent. Orion continued to watch as the warrior strode through the line of tents before disappearing on the other side of the small encampment.

Mindful of what Isha had told them about being overheard and closing the flap of the tent before speaking. "What do you think?" Kapian asked,

"That Magna is far more dangerous than I realized," Orion replied in a voice filled with resignation.

Jenny twisted onto her back and spread her arms, slowly sinking to the sandy bottom of the deep lagoon. All around her, colorful fish swam among the equally vivid coral reef where they lived. She drew in deep, calming breaths and watched the sunlight dance through the water.

She lay on the sand, running her fingers through the coarse granules while she thought of the conversation earlier. Drago, the Dragon King, had taken an unusual mate. Someone from another realm—like maybe Earth? Jenny wondered. Could that someone be Carly? If anyone could find a dragon and capture its heart, it would be Carly.

Jenny smiled at the idea. She could just imagine Carly falling off a cliff and into a dragon's lair. She knew Carly would bypass all the treasure and cuddle up with the dragon.

It's kind-of hard to burn something to a crisp if they have a death grip around your neck and are cooing all kinds of crazy things in your ear, Jenny thought.

And that was exactly what Carly would do. Jenny closed her eyes and imagined her best friend's reaction. She couldn't help but giggle at all the possibilities. Warmth flooded her, and deep down she knew that Carly was still alive. More than ever, Jenny was certain Carly had somehow found a magic portal and traveled through it. Now the question was: how could she get Orion to take her to the Isle of the Dragon to find out?

Jenny was running through possible ways of approaching Orion when she felt a movement in the water that was different from before. She stiffened and spread her fingers, focusing the way Orion taught her. She turned her head in the direction she thought the change was coming from, opened her eyes, and sat up.

She floated upward and waited as the shadowy figure of a man swam toward her. A frown creased her brow when she saw him pause several yards from her. Jenny didn't recognize the old man. He looked back at her with an expression of indecision, resignation, and hope.

Jenny's eyes widened in surprise when she saw an older woman behind him in what appeared to be a large, clear bubble. Glancing around, she realized that she had swum to the outer limits of the lagoon. Returning her focus to the man and woman, she noticed that they did not come any closer, but hovered on the edge where the reef dropped off.

"Who are you?" Jenny asked.

"I am Kell and this is my wife, Seline," the man introduced.

Jenny gazed at the old man. It was obvious that the he was from the Isle of the Sea Serpent. His short, white hair and vivid green eyes, and the fact that he was breathing underwater, made that plain to see. The woman reminded Jenny of someone. Her long black hair had touches of gray running through it, and her expression was tired and sad.

"My name is Jenny," she replied, tilting her head. "Have we met before?"

"No," the woman replied in a soft voice.

"That's funny. I feel like I know you from somewhere," Jenny murmured.

"Queen Jenny, we've come to ask for your help," Kell said.

"My help? What can I do?" Jenny asked in confusion.

"For our daughter, Magna," the woman explained.

"Magna!" Jenny exclaimed, jerking back in shock.

Tears filled the woman's eyes at her reaction. Kell turned and placed his hand on the clear bubble protecting the woman. Seline bowed her head and a soft sob escaped her. Kell murmured to her, and she shook her head.

"I told you that no one would understand," Seline whispered.

Jenny felt like a total heel. True, Magna might be horrible, but that didn't mean her parents were. Neither looked like they were a threat to her, and they had asked for help. It wasn't in Jenny to turn away someone in need, especially if there was anything that she could to do help them.

"Understand what?" Jenny asked, swimming closer.

Kell turned to look at Jenny with tired eyes. "When I saw the Sea King pass through our waters, I felt hope that he might be able to help us," he began.

"He will want to kill Magna just as everyone else wishes to," Seline bitterly said.

"Well, I can kind-of understand why. Magna has done some pretty bad things," Jenny ruefully responded. "I mean, you have to consider everything and not hold it against the people she is trying to destroy."

"It isn't her," Seline defended.

Jenny's skeptical expression must have been pretty clear. Seline became withdrawn, and defensively wrapped her arms around her waist before closing her eyes and whispering a series of words. Jenny blinked when the bubble dissolved, and both it and Seline disappeared.

"Where did she go?" Jenny asked in surprise.

"She returned to our home. What has happened has taken a heavy toll on her," Kell replied.

Jenny turned to the older man and placed her hand on his arm when he started to turn away in defeat. He still hadn't told her how she could help. That there was a common connection between what everyone was saying kept nagging at Jenny—this wasn't like the Magna they knew. Yes, it happened that people changed, but there were also clues, as if Magna was fighting whatever possessed her. Juno told her that Magna had helped him. That sounded more like the Magna from the stories that Orion and Kelia told about her.

"What can I do to help you?" she quietly asked.

Kell looked back at Jenny in surprise. His expression softened, and hope glimmered in his eyes. Deep down, Jenny knew she was making the right decision.

"Listen, keep an open mind, and try to believe what I am about to tell you," Kell said.

"I can do that," Jenny promised.

Kell drew in a deep breath and began telling Jenny a fantastic story that would have sounded more like a fairy tale than reality if she hadn't known that fairy tales do exist. It was a story of a happy young girl who chased after adventure and discovered something in the dark depths that would change her forever. The young woman was trapped inside her own body fighting to escape while being commanded and manipulated like a puppet, and she was desperate to right the wrongs that were done, knowing that ultimately the only way to do so was to die.

"Please, I know there is a way to save our daughter, Queen Jenny. Seline was able to talk to Magna briefly several months ago. She could see that Magna was reaching out for help. As a father, I beg you, ask the Sea King to find it in his heart to help us," Kell pleaded.

Jenny's heart broke. If she and Carly's parents had cared half as much about them as Kell and Seline cared about Magna, there was no telling what they could have accomplished. The paradox of that thought struck Jenny. If what happened to Carly was what she had hoped, then they both had exceeded anything that their parents could have ever dreamed.

"I will share with Orion what you've told me. I can't do more than that," she promised.

"Thank you. I must go. Someone approaches. Thank you again, Lady Jenny," Kell said.

Jenny nodded and watched Kell disappear over the edge of the reef. She felt movement in the water behind her. It was one of the guards. She could always feel the difference between them and Orion. With a sigh, she turned and began swimming back toward shore. It would appear she had a lot to share with Orion tonight.

CHAPTER TWENTY

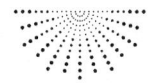

"There is a storm building," Orion warned, pulling back on Sea Fire's reins.

"I can feel the change in the currents, and the temperature is dropping," Jenny replied.

They had been traveling for several hours, nearly one hundred feet below the surface. Orion wished now he had followed his plan to return to the Isle of the Sea Serpent instead of traveling to the Isle of the Elementals. He would have if he had not felt the drastic change in the currents coming from the west. It had reminded him of the Pirate King's message.

The Elementals had always been a pain in Orion's backside. The King and Queen—hell, the Elemental people in general—had always been a strange lot. King Ruger had always been a little envious of Orion's ability to control water better than he could. Oh, they could make it rain and dance, but not much else.

Ruger had always complained that the Goddess gave the Elementals a mere taste of the powers of each kingdom without having it all. When Orion had asked how they related to the pirates, Queen Adrina had retorted that she had stolen Ruger's heart in a game of chance. It turned out Ruger had made a bet with Adrina that he could make it across one of the most forbidden areas on the Isle of the Monsters before she could. Adrina had saved Ruger's life and captured his heart—and Nali had promptly thrown both of them off the isle for upsetting the thunderbirds' nesting grounds.

"We will need to move deeper," Kapian said, coming up near them.

Orion cursed and glanced down. He could feel a dark turbulence ascending from beneath them. They were trapped. He pulled the trident free.

"What is it?" Jenny asked.

"I don't know," Orion said in a tight voice.

Out of the darkness, hundreds of dark shadows rose. Orion loudly cursed. Sea monkeys! The small but agile creatures came in two varieties—annoying and destructive. The only one who appeared to have any type of rapport with the damn things was Nali. The creatures normally stayed within the warm, shallow waters of one of the Isle of the Monsters' outer chain of islands.

"Look!" Kapian said, glancing up when a dark shadow passed overhead.

Orion's gaze briefly moved from the sea monkeys to the shape of several ships passing overhead. If that wasn't enough, a flash of lightning followed by the rolling sound of thunder reverberated through the water. Sea Fire twisted around, kicking and snapping at the sea monkeys as they swarmed around them. The water churned from the thrashing bodies, blocking his view of everyone and startling the sea dragons.

"Orion! Help!" Jenny cried out.

"Jenny!" Orion called.

"Orion, they have Jenny," Kapian shouted.

"Man the sails," Ashure Waves shouted above the roaring winds and rolling thunder.

"There is a gale forming, Cap'n," his first officer, Taupe LaBluff, said.

Ashure laughed. "Tell me something I don't already know," he shouted.

LaBluff was about to respond, probably with a depressing or negative comment, when the sound of horns began blowing. The smile on Ashure's face turned from one of excitement to one of grim determination. A second horn sounded. Ashure could already see the reason for the alarms—sea monkeys.

"Man your stations," LaBluff yelled. "All hands on deck! We are under attack!"

"Try not to kill the damn things!" Ashure yelled.

"But, Cap'n," LaBluff started to protest before he clamped his lips together and nodded. Turning, he repeated the order. "Drive them back into the sea!"

As much as Ashure would love to kill the damn things, he knew it would have to be a last resort. Nali, the Empress of the Isle of the Monsters, had an affinity with the annoying pests. Reaching for the new gun at his side, he gripped the helm of the Sea Wasp and turned it into the building waves.

The first of the sea monkeys made the mistake of climbing aboard from the bow of the ship. Ashure directed the ship into the wave. The bow dipped, cutting through the swell and washing the greedy bastards overboard. Their numerous legs were great for swimming, but unless they were able to latch onto something, they were clumsy on the polished decks.

"Ashure, behind you," LaBluff warned.

Ashure turned and aimed. He fired the pistol, and a high voltage of electricity hit the sea monkey in the chest. The creature shrieked in surprise and jumped overboard.

"I told you this was a good deal," Ashure chuckled to LaBluff.

His second in command grunted and continued trying to knock off the sea monkeys climbing up the side of the ship. There were far too many. The damn things smelled the treasure he had and wanted it.

"What has stirred them up?" LaBluff asked in exasperation when more took their place.

"I don't know. They are not usually so far from home," Ashure replied with a shrug.

A loud scream drew Ashure's attention. His gaze followed a struggle between two sea monkeys. The woman's fiery hair caught and held his attention. Motioning for LaBluff to take the wheel, Ashure stepped closer to the upper railing and watched as two crew members struck the offending sea monkeys who promptly released the woman.

She landed feet first on the deck, scrambled back from the railing and behind his men. Her back was pressed against the main mast, and she held onto the rigging with a white-knuckled grip. Lifting a hand to his tie, Ashure adjusted it and ran his tongue over his teeth, trying to remember what he had eaten for lunch and wishing he had brushed his teeth. After all, it wasn't every day that sea monkeys actually gave a treasure instead of stealing it.

"Where did she come from?" LaBluff asked in surprise.

"I don't know, but I'm about to find out," Ashure stated.

"Be careful, Captain. It might be the work of the Sea Witch," LaBluff warned.

Ashure ignored his second-in-command. He knew enough about deception to know when it was being used. His gut was telling him this woman had nothing to do with the Sea Witch.

Besides, he decided, if he took heed of every warning LaBluff gave him, he'd be sitting at home knitting for the rest of his days. Who knows? Even that could be dangerous if he were to slip and fall on a knitting needle. Life was about taking chances—about living it to the fullest—and about discovering new and exciting things.

"Hello. Ashure Waves, at your service, my beautiful fire-haired siren," he introduced himself with a lavish bow while shooting a sea monkey that had climbed over the railing behind him. "And you are…?" he asked with a charming grin.

If anyone had ever asked him what he expected the answer to be, it wouldn't have been to see stars—lots and lots of stars. In all honesty, he had been so focused on the woman's unusual eyes that he never saw her fist.

His head snapped back and he stumbled backwards several steps. The pistol he was holding fell to the deck when he released it to grab his poor, offended nose. It didn't help that the storm clouds suddenly opened up and heavy rain began to fall.

Ashure blinked and gently examined his nose with his fingers. He winced when he felt the swelling. It hurt, but he didn't think it was broken. He grimaced when he realized that while he'd been examining the stars of the heavens up close and personal, the fiery-haired maiden the sea monkeys had unintentionally dropped on his deck had retrieved his new toy and was aiming it at him.

"I'm Jenny," she said, waving the gun at him.

"Ah, Jenny from the sea. You may not look like the others of your kind, but I have to say you hit like one. I should have known better than to take a sea monkey's gift," Ashure complained.

"Step aside, and I'll be out of your hair," Jenny warned, waving the gun again.

Ashure waved his hand at her. "You may want to look behind you first," he suggested.

The woman released a startled scream when a sea monkey hung down off the mast at face level. She twisted, her finger closing around the trigger, and fell back into his waiting arms when the pistol discharged a stream of electricity. The sea monkey and a good chunk of the mast were thrown back across the deck before disappearing into the rough sea below.

"It has a bit of kick if you aren't expecting it," Ashure said, deftly taking the gun out of her hands.

"What the hell was that?" Jenny asked, pulling free of Ashure's arms.

"The sea monkey or my new toy? I won it off a Cyclops during a game of chance," Ashure said, shooting another sea monkey.

"I know a Cyclops named Cyan," Jenny murmured.

"Really? Her mate Boost and I go back a long way. Did they have that crusty Minotaur with them?" Ashure asked.

"Meir?" Jenny said, glancing over her shoulder. "Oh, there's another one!"

Ashure turned and fired low from the hip. "That's the one. Never play a game of cards with him. He totally destroyed the pub when he lost," he warned.

"Oh, okay," Jenny murmured.

"Jenny!"

"Orion!! These are sea monkeys! Real, live sea monkeys. They are bigger than the ones back home," Jenny said, weaving her way unsteadily toward Orion and Kapian.

Ashure sighed. Once again, it would appear he was a day too late. First Drago and now Orion. It would seem his luck always took a turn for the worse when it came to finding fascinating women.

"Hello, Orion," Ashure called.

"Ashure. It would appear you have an infestation issue," Orion responded with a grin.

"Ha-ha. Don't kill any of them. Nali will be upset," Ashure warned.

"I won't," Orion responded, lifting the trident and aiming a funnel of water at a line of the creatures crawling over the railing.

The loud crackle of electricity and the sound of thunder shattering the air drew Ashure's attention to the sky. Raising a hand to his hair, he felt the static electricity building up. That could only mean one thing —thunderbirds.

"We've got company," Ashure shouted.

"I know," Orion replied, sending another dozen sea monkeys back into the ocean.

Ashure watched as a huge airship with twelve thunderbirds emerged from the dark, heavy clouds. Lightning flashed from the clouds to the birds. It was a marvelously breathtaking, and an absolutely terrifying, phenomenon to behold.

The form of a woman could be seen standing on the railing. When the airship was even with the Sea Wasp, the figure dove off the railing. Ashure's breath caught at the splendid and very dramatic entrance of Nali, Empress of the Isle of the Monsters. She twirled as she descended, her arms opening, and long wings caught the air. She landed on the polished deck of his ship, one knee slightly bent and a sword in her hand.

Ashure casually tucked his gun inside his coat and gave Nali his most dashing smile. The smile grew strained when she continued to stare at him with unblinking eyes as she straightened. A hint of uncertainty flashed through his eyes, and he mentally replayed how much she could have seen. His chin rose when she lifted the sword until the flat part of it rested against his skin. Her brow creased into a dark frown, and she gave him a puzzled look.

"Who broke your nose?" Nali asked.

CHAPTER TWENTY-ONE

Orion's lips twitched at Ashure's sour expression. For the past hour, Ashure had been arguing that Nali should be responsible for his lost inventory. Orion had to admit that Ashure had a point—about the size of a pinhead, but he did have a point when the Pirate King reminded Nali that she was responsible for the sea monkeys since they were under her jurisdiction.

"So, you want me to compensate you for the stolen items that you stole in the first place?" Nali asked with a raised eyebrow.

"Finally! You understand," Ashure replied.

Jenny's soft giggle drew a smile from Orion. He couldn't resist caressing her shoulder where his hand rested. They were currently sitting in Ashure's meeting room below decks. The glossy dark wood with gold accents, jewel encrusted lamps, and plush red velvet chairs and couch, not to mention the imported marble inlaid, magic-fed fireplace, proved that Ashure was either an excellent pirate or a cunning businessman.

"You could have at least thanked me for shooing all of the sea monkeys away first. Then, I might have considered it. Now, I will just take back the volt pistol that you cheated out of my Cyclops," Nali said, rolling her head back to look up at Ashure with a serene smile. "I'll also take a case of this brandy as a thank you."

The scowl on Ashure's face grew darker before he softly chuckled and his eyes danced with merriment. He picked up the bottle of whiskey he had been about to pour, walked over, and placed it in front of Nali. Bending over, he brushed a quick kiss across her lips before twisting away when she jerked upright.

"I'll give you half a bottle of my best whiskey and take the kiss as payment," he teased.

"One day, Ashure, you'll meet a woman who will tame your flamboyant soul," Nali warned before picking up the bottle he placed in front of her, refilling her glass, and taking a sip. "This is good, but I still like the brandy better."

Jenny bent her head close to Orion. "Is he always like this?" she asked under her breath.

"Yes. This is why everyone wants to kill him, especially Drago," Orion replied.

Ashure pointed his finger at Orion. "Drago does not want to kill me. Well, maybe he does, but Carly adores me, as do their children. I send them gifts," he said.

Orion groaned when Jenny sat forward in her chair. Her eyes glowed, and the smile on her face grew until he swore it rivaled the sun. Her hands gripped the table, and he could feel the excitement in her growing.

"Carly... As in Carly Tate? She has light brown hair and brown eyes and is about this tall and...," Jenny exclaimed, talking rapidly as she described her best friend.

"Yes, yes, and yes. She is most delightful, a bit on the dangerous side if you aren't careful, but totally delightful. I have no idea why she refuses to leave that grumpy old dragon," Ashure said. "I offered her the world, and all she had eyes for was a stupid, but exceedingly wealthy, fire-breathing dragon."

"Which you are lucky wasn't breathing fire when he looked at you," Nali chuckled. Sobering, she leaned forward and looked at Orion. "Magna has to be stopped, Orion."

Orion leaned forward and rested his elbows on the table. He nodded to Nali, knowing that the time had finally come for the true reasons for her being there. Magna's dark reach had once again spread throughout each of the isles of the Seven Kingdoms.

"I will take care of her once and for all," Orion vowed.

Nali and Ashure were both shaking their heads. "You cannot do this on your own. You will need Drago's help, but he must not kill her," Nali said.

"Stop her, but don't kill her. I can see Orion being able to do that, but Drago…? I think that is asking for a lot, Nali. You know what she did to his people," Ashure warned.

Nali shot Ashure a hot glare. "I know what the mirror has told me. Carly has started a chain of events that will lead to Magna's downfall, but the time is not right," she argued.

"Time is not right…? What do you want Magna to do? Take over half the kingdoms? The Elementals have already run scared and changed the seas. Orion, you must surely have felt the imbalance," Ashure said, placing his hands on the table and leaning toward Orion.

"Yes. I can control the changes for now. Ashure has a point, Nali. There will come a time and a place when I will have a chance to stop Magna, and I will do it," Orion said in a grim voice.

"Orion," Jenny whispered, wanting to protest, but understanding that there wasn't a lot she could do to help Kell and Seline if Magna caused any more damage.

Orion reached over and cupped Jenny's hand. "I will do what needs to be done. If there is a way to save her, I will," he promised.

"Great! You want to save her, Drago wants to kill her, and Nali wants to wait until the time is right. I need another drink," Ashure groaned.

"Don't forget my case of brandy!" Nali reminded him.

∼

Later that evening, Jenny sat on a stool brushing her hair. Ashure had invited them to stay for the night. Jenny, eager to hear more about Carly's adventures had agreed before Orion could say no. Orion had reluctantly agreed, much to the amusement of Nali.

The evening had been amazing for Jenny. While the pirate ships might look like something out of a swashbuckling movie on the outside, they were nothing like it on the inside. Lush and filled with all the modern conveniences, the Sea Wasp reminded Jenny more of a luxury cruise ship below decks. A decadent dinner followed by drinks and Ashure's eloquent storytelling had made for a delightful evening.

"You are still smiling," Orion complained. "He was not that entertaining."

"Yes, he was," Jenny laughed, gazing at where Orion was lying in bed.

"I can be more entertaining," he suggested.

Jenny saw the wicked gleam in his eyes. Deciding two could play that game, she lay the hairbrush down on the vanity table in front of her. Reaching up, she slowly pushed the borrowed silk dressing gown off her shoulders. She was rewarded by Orion's loud hiss of appreciation.

"I forgot to put on the nightgown—and panties," she said, slowly standing up so the dressing gown pooled around her feet. "Oops."

"Goddess, Jenny. Remind me to install mirrors in the hut," Orion choked out.

Jenny felt the power of her effect on Orion and reveled in it. The knowledge that she was loved and that she loved him swept away any feelings of doubt. They were the perfect match. Lifting her hands, she cupped her breasts.

"Come here," Orion ordered, throwing back the covers to reveal his throbbing cock.

"Do you like what you see?" Jenny teased, pinching her nipples to make them harder.

"You know I do," Orion replied, his gaze following the movements of her fingers. He licked his lips. "I can make them hard for you."

Jenny's right hand slid down to the red curls between her legs. She stroked her finger across her swelling clitoris. Orion's gaze was glued to the reflection in the mirror.

"Can you make this wet?" she asked, tilting her head to the side.

Orion softly cursed and quickly slid out of the bed, and the giggle Jenny was about to utter turned into a choked cry of arousal when he wrapped one arm around her waist and the other under her knees. He swung her up into his arms and turned toward the bed.

Jenny felt the silky material of the bedding under her back as he laid her down. Her eyelids drooped with desire when he climbed over her until he was straddling her chest. Bending forward, he wrapped his hand in her hair. The movement aligned his hard cock with her mouth. He reached behind with his other hand and tweaked her nipple.

Her lips parted, and he pushed his hips forward. His cock slowly slid into her warm mouth. Jenny rolled her tongue around his bulbous head, tasting his pre-cum and savoring the pleasure of being held captive in his embrace as much as he was in hers.

"Suck it," he murmured.

Jenny's throaty hum of agreement pulled a hiss from Orion. Realizing the effect she was having on him, she raised her hands to add to the torture. Using her lips, tongue, and hands, she made love to his cock and heavy sack. She gently kneaded his balls with one hand while using the other hand to massage his taut buttocks. She had discovered that he had a relatively small amount of body hair the first time they made love. It made sense when she thought about the professional swimmers back home. Hair could create a drag in the water. The sea people had evolved to have very little hair besides that on their head. The light coating Orion had on his arms and legs was very fine and light in color.

Jenny didn't mind. She had been around enough professional swimmers during her years as a lifeguard to know that hair does not necessarily make the man. Running her hands up his smooth butt cheeks to the crack of his ass, she teased it. He rewarded her by throwing his head back and rocking his hips. His cock slid in and out of her mouth, growing fuller.

"My turn," he suddenly said.

"But...," Jenny groaned in frustration when he pulled his cock out of her mouth and slid down her body. "I... Oh, yeah."

∼

Orion knew if he didn't stop, he would come in Jenny's mouth. Bending down, he picked up her legs and placed them over his shoulders. This position opened her for his tongue. She reached down and spread her lips, opening up for him. He could see the small, swollen clit. He loved how when he pleasured her there, she would lose control until she came. Leaning forward, he began his quest to bring her pleasure.

Her body stiffened at the first touch of his tongue. The tip of his tongue caressed her swollen clit, pulling a low, guttural cry from her. Clamping his lips around it, he began an assault that drove Jenny wild. Her loud cry echoed through the room. She pulled her hands away and lifted them to grip the headboard. Orion loved how her body twisted and turned, fighting to break free from his touch. He wrapped his hands around her thighs and held her in a tight grip as he nipped and stroked her with his tongue. Her gasping cries drove him on until a rush of her warm juices filled his mouth.

Releasing her, he sat up and gripped her hips. He turned her and pulled her up onto her knees. Positioning himself, he bent over her and drove his cock into her still pulsing channel. Jenny pressed her face into the pillow to smother her scream. Her body, over-sensitive from her orgasm, reacted by coating his cock with her hot cum.

Orion, half mad with need, grunted and pinched her nipples. He pressed his cock inside her as deep as it could go. Rocking back and forth, he felt her body greedily sucking him in. The nerve in his jaw throbbed as he tried to hold on as long as he could. Reaching down between her legs, he played with her swollen clit until her head jerked up, and she pressed back against him as she came again, her gasping sobs revealing the intensity of her orgasm.

His body tightened, his ballsack so hard he was afraid it would explode. When the pressure finally reached critical level, he rocked his hips forward, digging his fingers into her soft flesh and releasing the floodgates, which were holding back the dam of his seed, into her in a long wave of ecstasy.

Their bodies melted down to the bed, his body wrapped around her and his cock still firmly buried inside her. Orion felt Jenny release a shuddering breath before her body relaxed. He softly chuckled when he heard a soft snore a few minutes later. Their long journey, the excitement of the day, and their intense lovemaking had finally overwhelmed her.

Orion lay holding her until he was sure she was in a deep sleep. He carefully pulled free, smiling when she released an unconscious groan of disappointment. Rising from the bed, he went to the bathroom and cleaned up before bringing back a warm cloth and towel to clean Jenny. Tossing the items into a basket when he was finished, he climbed back into bed and pulled Jenny back into his arms.

His mind wandered while his body began to relax. He smiled when he thought of Jenny's teasing. It had driven him wild. His smile faded when he thought of Ashure. One of these days that damn pirate was going to meet his match. Orion hoped that he was around to witness it when that happened.

Ashure's constant flirting, earlier in the evening, had left Orion wanting to kill the pirate king. If Ashure had given Jenny one more seductive smile, Orion swore he would drown the man the first chance he got. It didn't matter that Ashure had been the perfect gentleman and host in all other aspects.

Of course, Nali's knowing looks of amusement had been almost as bad as well as the quiet reminders that Ashure was like this with everyone. Orion didn't care if the pirate king had a reputation as a rogue and a flirt; the man had no business flirting with his woman. Jenny had ignored Ashure's overtures and spent most of the time chatting with Nali when Ashure wasn't trying to dazzle her with his stories of adventures. In the end, Ashure had given up and only talked about Carly and Drago before Orion finally decided it was time to call it a night.

One of these days, Ashure, Orion thought as sleep began to pull at him, *I really hope Drago, Nali, and I are there to see it.*

∼

Early the next morning, Orion was making the same wish he had the night before. Standing near the railing of the ship, he glanced up as Nali shouted down a reminder. He waved his hand in acknowledgement.

"I know, capture Magna, and don't kill her. I'll know when the time is right," Orion muttered with a shake of his head.

"She is as cryptic as ever. I swear she makes up half the stuff," Ashure remarked.

"She has the mirror of the Goddess. She sees things that we don't," Orion reminded Ashure.

Ashure shrugged. "Sometimes you see things that aren't what you think," he retorted.

Orion frowned. He hadn't missed the slightly bitter smile or biting tone in Ashure's remark. The sound of footsteps pulled his attention to

Jenny. She was walking across the deck and chatting with Kapian. Something his friend said made Jenny laugh.

"You are a very fortunate man, Orion. I hope you appreciate the gift you have been given," Ashure quietly murmured.

Orion glanced at the pirate king in surprise. Ashure was staring at Jenny with a shuttered expression. Once again, he saw a part of Ashure that he had not seen before. Ashure's expression changed the moment Jenny looked their way. The easy smile and flirty manner were back in place, making Orion wonder if he had imagined Ashure's moodiness a moment ago.

"I have never in my life had someone so beautiful walk the plank before," Ashure said, grasping Jenny's hand and bowing over it before he pressed a kiss to the back of it and stepped back. "Parting with you will be a very sweet sorrow. I truly hope we will meet again."

Jenny laughed. "I'm sure we will, and I'm not walking the plank, I'm jumping overboard," she teased. She stepped forward and gave Ashure a hug and a kiss. "Thank you for telling me about Carly. I can't wait to see if it really is her," she quietly added with a sincere smile.

Pulling back, she lifted her hand before she turned and walked over to the side where the railing had been removed. She balanced on the edge for a brief second before diving off and disappearing beneath the waves. Kapian followed a second later.

Ashure turned and grinned at Orion. "I love a woman with a sense of humor," he chuckled, watching as Jenny gracefully disappeared over the side.

"I hope you get one with a healthy dose because she'll need it to put up with you," Orion remarked. "Send word if you hear anything of Magna. I will do the same."

"I will, my friend. I'm sure I can convince a sea monkey or minnow to deliver a message," Ashure dryly retorted, watching as Orion disappeared over the side.

"Where to now, Captain?" LaBluff asked.

Ashure was thoughtful for a moment before he smiled. "We have not paid the King of the Giants a visit in a while. Let us see if Koorgan is in a more favorable temper to receive some guests," he said.

LaBluff drew in a deep breath and released it with a shake of his head. "Yes, Captain. Pull up your big-boy pants, men. We are heading for the Isle of the Giants," he announced to a chorus of groans.

Ashure didn't bother trying to contain his amusement. Some would think that the Isle of the Giants would belong under Nali's domain, but these were not your typical monsters. His mind rifled through his inventory of treasure as he considered what he could use as a bargaining tool.

"Fill the sails, men. LaBluff, did Nali leave behind any of that brandy she likes so much?" Ashure yelled.

EPILOGUE

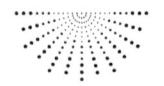

A week later:

Jenny slowly emerged from the sea. Apprehension and hope churned in her stomach as she curled her toes in the coarse, black sand. She glanced anxiously behind her. She knew Orion was coming. It was kind-of hard to miss it when every fish in the sea was warning her—not to mention Dolph and Juno.

"Do you see her?" Juno called from behind her.

Jenny shook her head and waved her hand at the little boy. Releasing the breath she was holding in, she pushed her wet hair away from her face and turned to look up at the palace on the cliff above.

"Do you want me to sneak in? I can climb up there," Dolph offered.

Jenny laughed and lifted a hand to rub her temple. Yes, she should have waited for Orion to return, but she couldn't stand it any longer. It felt like she had been waiting forever to find out what had happened to Carly and to make sure she was okay. They had been back home for a week—a full week—and Orion had been gone all but the first day so there had been no chance of going—at least with him—unless she was willing to wait even longer.

"I should never have listened to the boys. They are kids. What was I thinking?" Jenny groaned.

Jenny had been mumbling about the different ways to find out if Drago's Carly was her Carly. The boys had heard her and decided they were going to help her slip out. It had been hard to do that since Orion had given Kapian and Kelia strict instructions that they were to protect her while he attended a meeting with the King and Queen of the Elementals. Jenny had offered to stay with the boys when Juno broke down in tears, heartbroken that he didn't have a baby sister yet and complaining that it was taking forever to make her.

Jenny quickly learned that Dolph and Juno could charm a dragon out of his gold, and they were even more slippery than Ashure in a game of chance. The boys had planned their escape with a precision that would have impressed the best military general. They knew that timing was essential, supplies a necessity, and a map was only needed if you didn't know where you were planning to go. They knew all three, and before Kelia had closed the door to their living quarters with a goodnight wish, they were slipping through the back garden gate.

Now it was early morning, and the sun was just lighting the sky. Jenny had only taken a few steps onto the beach when she heard Orion call out to her to stop. He was a lot faster—and closer—than she had calculated. With a soft groan, she turned and watched as he rose up out of the waves to join her on the beach.

"Jenny, stop! Come back into the water. Now, before he gets any closer," Orion ordered in a low, husky voice filled with worry.

"Orion… Carly…," Jenny started to argue, turning to see her husband wading toward her.

"I know how much you miss her, Jenny. Return to the water with the boys. I will face Drago and ask him if he knows if his Carly is your lost friend. This is too dangerous for you, especially now," Orion insisted.

"I know it has to be my Carly, Orion," Jenny replied in a pleading voice. "I can feel it."

"Who dares to come into my kingdom?" a rough, thundering voice roared.

She started to turn back when she saw a shadow suddenly pass over them. Shielding her eyes, her breath caught on the outline of what could only be a 'mythical' dragon. Her lips parted in awe at the sight of the creature.

"Drago!" Orion snarled back, raising the trident in his hand in warning.

Jenny stumbled back several feet. Water lapped around her ankles, and she remained frozen, afraid to move. The ground shook as the massive dragon landed with ease a few feet from where they were standing. The creature dug a front claw into the ground, which was as black as he was, and scraped the sand. She gripped Orion when he roughly pulled her behind him.

"We come in peace, Drago," Orion snapped. "You are frightening my wife."

"Your wife," Drago said, turning his head to gaze down at Jenny with blazing golden eyes. "I was told Shamill was dead. This is not Shamill."

"No, this is…," Orion started to say.

Jenny's eyes widened when a smaller dragon landed beside Drago. She could tell the large male was unhappy about her being there from the way he was trying to shield her with his massive wings. The female ignored him, locking her gaze on Jenny.

"Jenny?" the female dragon whispered before she drew in a deep breath and transformed. "Jenny, is that really you?"

"Oh, Carly! I knew it! I knew you weren't dead," Jenny cried, surging forward before Orion could stop her. "I knew you weren't dead. I missed you so much."

Drago looked at the two women crying and embracing before looking back toward Orion, the trident now by his side. His claws curled into the sand. Resigned that he wasn't going to be eating anyone today, he shifted. Orion gave him a pained expression before shaking his head.

"Is this the Jenny that Carly is always talking about?" Drago asked with a scowl.

"What do you think?" Orion dryly asked.

Drago glanced at Orion and grunted. "From the way they are crying and talking non-stop, I'd have to say yes. Carly wished to return to her world to let Jenny know that she was safe, but the passage was sealed," he reluctantly admitted.

"Jenny was devastated by Carly's disappearance. She never stopped believing that she was alive. She hoped that Carly had somehow ended up in our world. I was afraid to break her heart even more," Orion confessed.

"I understand. I felt the same way. But now we don't have to worry about that," Drago said, slapping Orion on the shoulder.

"Daddy, can we come out now?" several voices echoed in unison.

"That's right! You have children. Ashure told me about them," Orion chuckled.

Drago's face flushed with pride when three young dragons peeked out from under a nearby bush. He emitted a soft growl under his breath, and they piled out, squealing and bouncing toward Carly and Jenny. With an exasperated sigh, Drago folded his arms across his chest and nodded.

"Yes, and they listen about as good as my mate does. I told them to stay," he grumbled. "How are your sons?"

"Listening about as well as your three," Orion admitted, turning to raise his hand.

Within seconds, Dolph and Juno were hurriedly wading up onto the beach. They grinned at Drago and their father as they flashed by, heading toward his kids. Drago had to admit that having other children to play with would be good for the kids.

"You know, if you added a little girl, it would make my life a little easier," Drago suggested. "My princess needs a playmate."

Orion grinned and chuckled. "There will be in a few months," he informed Drago in a quiet voice. "Jenny wants to name our daughter Carly."

The men watched the women sink down onto the coarse sand to play with the excited dragons. Dolph and Juno laughed when the boys shifted in excitement.

Drago started forward when his tiny daughter released a low cry after she fell face first in the sand. Drago paused when Jenny tenderly picked the little girl up in her arms and rubbed her cheek against the child's head.

"You have a good wife," Drago observed. "She will make my mate happy. You may stay."

∼

Orion chuckled. Drago was looking just too damn proud of himself. He had to admit that it was good to see the other man happy. Drago deserved to find happiness after everything he had lost. If Orion had his way, he would find a way to reverse the spell that Magna had cast. He shook his head. Today was not the day to dwell on his cousin. Instead, he imagined the battle Drago would have fought with the women—and the kids—if he tried to prevent them from seeing each other again.

"Good, because you would have been fighting the battle of separating the women on your own," Orion replied with an amused grin. "You do know that this means the end of our feud, don't you? All Jenny talked about was her friend, Carly. Now that she knows she is here, I have a feeling we are going to be frequent visitors."

"Make sure you bring the boys when you come. My kids enjoy having yours to play with instead of me," Drago shrugged. "The boys have begged me to find others their age, but I honestly didn't know any. I had forgotten that you had two; otherwise I would have kidnapped them years ago. I will warn you that my little Jenny likes to have tea with her dragons. She makes her brothers and me play with her. It looks like she has taken a shine to your youngest boy."

Orion chuckled. It sounded like Drago was taking his fatherly responsibilities to heart. He could relate to how much joy being a father could bring.

He glanced at Juno who was building a sandcastle with little Jenny. His son looked up at him and smiled. Orion didn't miss the look of expectation on Juno's face. Nodding his head, he let Juno know that his wish would come true soon.

Orion turned his gaze to Jenny's glowing face. He felt love surge through him as he watched her tilt her head back and laugh at something Carly said. As fearful as he had been earlier, he was glad things had worked out. He was happy that she had found her friend.

He acknowledged that Jenny and Carly's friendship would help forge a new alliance between him and Drago. That alliance would speed the healing process that kept the kingdoms from reaching their full potential. There was still much to do, but the Seven Kingdoms were once again on a path to peace.

Orion's thoughts briefly flashed to Magna. As far as he knew, she was unaware that he now had both Eyes of the Sea Serpent. So far, his search for Magna had been fruitless. If she was not in the water, it would be difficult to locate her. His brief visit to the Isle of the Elements proved that fear of Magna's growing strength was having severe negative effects. His only hope was that she would return to the water where he could capture her.

"Orion, Carly asked us to stay for dinner. I told her yes. We are also staying for a few days," Jenny called out to him with a happy grin.

"Ah, the visiting stage has begun. Carly warned me that such a day would arrive. I believe she called them slumber parties," Drago groaned.

"Jenny told me of doing such things with Carly when she was growing up. She has taught the boys how to build forts. They love sleeping in them at night and playing in them during the day," Orion chuckled.

He bent and scooped up little Jenny in his arms when she toddled over to him and held up her arms. Orion grinned when the little girl shook her head and wound her arms around his neck when her father tried to take her. Drago's soft snort of wounded pride drew a giggle from his daughter.

"Betrayed already," Drago sighed. "The forts are already made. We cannot keep the covers on their beds at the moment. Mine also love to have nightly pillow fights. I suspect they will be camping out together tonight."

"Most definitely, and preferably in your living quarters," Orion chuckled.

"How about we have a challenge to see who gets the kids? I wouldn't mind a few nights alone with my mate," Drago suggested with a hopeful grin.

Orion shook his head. "There is no way I'm playing a game of chance after being around Ashure. How about we flip a coin and take turns?" he suggested instead.

Drago was quiet for a moment while he thought about it. "Heads, you get them, tails we do," he agreed.

"Little Jenny tosses," Orion said.

Drago grunted and pulled a gold coin from his pocket. He gave it to Orion to look at. Orion noticed the markings were different on each side and nodded. He handed it to Little Jenny who promptly stuffed it in her pocket.

"I should have known better," Drago groaned with a shake of his head. "Never give a dragon gold. She won't give it up now."

"I have an idea," Orion said with a grin. "Jenny, Carly, heads or tails?"

"Tails," both women said at the same time. "Why?"

Orion grinned. "The boys are spending the night with Drago and Carly," he replied.

Drago scowled at Orion. "I think you set me up," he said suspiciously.

"At least you didn't lose another gold coin over it," Orion laughed.

∽

Orion quietly closed the door to their bedroom. Jenny turned from where she was standing on the outside balcony. A gentle sea breeze was blowing in, and her hair floated around her shoulders.

"Are the boys settled?" she asked.

Orion chuckled. "I suspect they will be up all night. They discovered Drago's magical paper birds and want him to make some fish. It took a while to get them to understand that paper and water do not mix well. Drago is currently trying different combinations of magic to see if he can create some. I never thought I would see that mighty dragon melt into a pile of molten lava," he admitted.

Jenny smiled and turned back to look out over the walls of the castle. Orion could feel her sadness. Walking over to her, he wrapped his arms around her and drew her back against him. She released a deep sigh and laid her hands over his, caressing him.

"What's wrong?" Orion asked, brushing a kiss against her temple.

Jenny shook her head. "I don't know how Drago could have survived. Carly told me what happened to his people and what it means for a dragon. I'm glad she found him. No one deserves to be so alone," she whispered, lifting a hand to brush away the tear that ran down her cheek.

Orion didn't say anything. He had felt it the moment the dragons disappeared and Drago retreated—all the kingdoms had. Despite everything, Drago and Carly had filled their kingdom with warmth and laughter. Even now, they could hear the echo of it ringing through the palace as Drago playfully growled, and the children squealed in delight.

"Carly has filled Drago's life just as you have filled mine. You can be surrounded by people and still be alone, Jenny. When I am with you, I never feel alone," Orion admitted.

Jenny turned in his arms. Her eyes were filled with love. Orion lifted his hand to caress her cheek.

"I love you, Orion," she murmured, leaning closer to him.

"How about showing me how much?" he suggested.

"With pleasure, my merman," Jenny purred, threading her fingers through his short hair with one hand while her other hand moved down his body.

Orion captured her lips in a passionate kiss, their breaths mingling and growing more urgent. He picked Jenny up and turned toward the bed as the sound of Drago's yell rang out behind him.

"You owe me, Sea King! Ouch! No bite, Jen," Drago roared.

"Pillow attack!" the boys yelled.

Orion caught the door with his heel and shut out the sound of Drago's torture. Tonight was his and Jenny's, and he was going to cherish every single second of it.

"Goddess, but I will love you forever, my beautiful mermaid," Orion moaned.

Seven Kingdoms—Eight Incredible Love Stories…
Check out what's next in the series:

A Witch's Touch

As the darkness spreads, help comes when she needs it the most...

Marina Fae never considered herself a powerful witch or dreamed that she could make a difference in the fight to save her people, but when the Sea Witch's magic swept across the Isle of Magic, Marina led a group of children to safety, and it was the only the beginning of what she discovered she can do.

Detective Mike Hallbrook's search for two women who disappeared in Yachats State Park seems like it is going nowhere until suddenly he finds himself on an unfamiliar beach rescuing a woman from a creature straight out of a horror movie!

Marina and Mike must work together to save the Isle of Magic and the rest of the kingdoms, but as the Sea Witch's evil spreads, they know they cannot stop her alone...

Check out the full book here: books2read.com/AWitchsTouch

Or read on to discover a new series!

The Beast Prince, *A Fairy Tale Novella*

Lisa Tootles discovers more than she expects when she steps through an enchanted doorway during a game of Manhunt with her cousins. On the other side is a Prince that has been cursed.

Sharden is running out of time. Cursed before he was even born, he waits by the doorway for the one the witch said could break the spell. What he gets is a curvy human woman who doesn't have a clue that his world even existed, much less how to break a curse.

Check out the full novella here: books2read.com/The-Beast-Prince

ADDITIONAL BOOKS

If you loved this story by me (S.E. Smith) please leave a review! You can discover additional books at: http://sesmithfl.com and http://sesmithya.com or find your favorite way to keep in touch here: https://sesmithfl.com/contact-me/ Be sure to sign up for my newsletter to hear about new releases!

Recommended Reading Order Lists:

http://sesmithfl.com/reading-list-by-events/

http://sesmithfl.com/reading-list-by-series/

The Series

Science Fiction / Romance

Dragon Lords of Valdier Series

It all started with a king who crashed on Earth, desperately hurt. He inadvertently discovered a species that would save his own.

Curizan Warrior Series

The Curizans have a secret, kept even from their closest allies, but even they are not immune to the draw of a little known species from an isolated planet called Earth.

Marastin Dow Warriors Series

The Marastin Dow are reviled and feared for their ruthlessness, but not all want to live a life of murder. Some wait for just the right time to escape....

Sarafin Warriors Series

A hilariously ridiculous human family who happen to be quite formidable... and a secret hidden on Earth. The origin of the Sarafin species is more than it seems. Those cat-shifting aliens won't know what hit them!

Dragonlings of Valdier Novellas

The Valdier, Sarafin, and Curizan Lords had children who just cannot stop getting into trouble! There is nothing as cute or funny as magical, shapeshifting kids, and nothing as heartwarming as family.

Cosmos' Gateway Series

Cosmos created a portal between his lab and the warriors of Prime. Discover new worlds, new species, and outrageous adventures as secrets are unravelled and bridges are crossed.

The Alliance Series

When Earth received its first visitors from space, the planet was thrown into a panicked chaos. The Trivators came to bring Earth into the Alliance of Star Systems, but now they must take control to prevent the humans from destroying themselves. No one was prepared for how the humans will affect the Trivators, though, starting with a family of three sisters....

Lords of Kassis Series

It began with a random abduction and a stowaway, and yet, somehow, the Kassisans knew the humans were coming long before now. The fate of more than one world hangs in the balance, and time is not always linear....

Zion Warriors Series

Time travel, epic heroics, and love beyond measure. Sci-fi adventures with heart and soul, laughter, and awe-inspiring discovery...

Paranormal / Fantasy / Romance

Magic, New Mexico Series

Within New Mexico is a small town named Magic, an... unusual town, to say the least. With no beginning and no end, spanning genres, authors, and universes, hilarity and drama combine to keep you on the edge of your seat!

Spirit Pass Series

There is a physical connection between two times. Follow the stories of those who travel back and forth. These westerns are as wild as they come!

Second Chance Series

Stand-alone worlds featuring a woman who remembers her own death. Fiery and mysterious, these books will steal your heart.

More Than Human Series

Long ago there was a war on Earth between shifters and humans. Humans lost, and today they know they will become extinct if something is not done....

The Fairy Tale Series

A twist on your favorite fairy tales!

A Seven Kingdoms Tale

Long ago, a strange entity came to the Seven Kingdoms to conquer and feed on their life force. It found a host, and she battled it within her body for centuries while destruction and devastation surrounded her. Our story begins when the end is near, and a portal is opened....

Epic Science Fiction / Action Adventure

Project Gliese 581G Series

An international team leave Earth to investigate a mysterious object in our solar system that was clearly made by someone, someone who isn't from Earth. Discover new worlds and conflicts in a sci-fi adventure sure to become your favorite!

New Adult / Young Adult

Breaking Free Series

A journey that will challenge everything she has ever believed about herself as danger reveals itself in sudden, heart-stopping moments.

The Dust Series

Fragments of a comet hit Earth, and Dust wakes to discover the world as he knew it is gone. It isn't the only thing that has changed, though, so has Dust...

ABOUT THE AUTHOR

S.E. Smith is an *internationally acclaimed, New York Times* **and** *USA TODAY Bestselling* author of science fiction, romance, fantasy, paranormal, and contemporary works for adults, young adults, and children. She enjoys writing a wide variety of genres that pull her readers into worlds that take them away.

Printed in Great Britain
by Amazon